# THE INDOMITABLE SILENCE

A Man's Quest for the Heart's Fierce Whisper

## ANGELO MEIJERS

BALBOA PRESS

A DIVISION OF HAY HOUSE

Copyright © 2018 Angelo Meijers.

All rights reserved. No part of this book may be used or reproduced by any means, graphic, electronic, or mechanical, including photocopying, recording, taping or by any information storage retrieval system without the written permission of the author except in the case of brief quotations embodied in critical articles and reviews.

Balboa Press books may be ordered through booksellers or by contacting:

Balboa Press
A Division of Hay House
1663 Liberty Drive
Bloomington, IN 47403
www.balboapress.com
1 (877) 407-4847

Because of the dynamic nature of the Internet, any web addresses or links contained in this book may have changed since publication and may no longer be valid. The views expressed in this work are solely those of the author and do not necessarily reflect the views of the publisher, and the publisher hereby disclaims any responsibility for them.

The author of this book does not dispense medical advice or prescribe the use of any technique as a form of treatment for physical, emotional, or medical problems without the advice of a physician, either directly or indirectly. The intent of the author is only to offer information of a general nature to help you in your quest for emotional and spiritual well-being. In the event you use any of the information in this book for yourself, which is your constitutional right, the author and the publisher assume no responsibility for your actions.

Any people depicted in stock imagery provided by Getty Images are models, and such images are being used for illustrative purposes only. Certain stock imagery © Getty Images.

Print information available on the last page.

ISBN: 978-1-9822-0592-8 (sc)
ISBN: 978-1-9822-0590-4 (hc)
ISBN: 978-1-9822-0591-1 (e)

Library of Congress Control Number: 2018906677

Balboa Press rev. date: 06/08/2018

Front cover and back cover photo credits:
Felix Kortrijk
website:www.shortrich.nl


Keywords:
Self-actualization, Spirituality, Heart

... to my Mum, for loving me as only a mother can.

# CONTENTS

Acknowledgements ................................................................. xi

Foreword ........................................................................... xiii

Intro ..................................................................................... 1

A Letter ............................................................................... 5

The Cabin ........................................................................... 29

A Lamp Burns ..................................................................... 51

Tears in Heaven .................................................................. 75

The City of Lights ............................................................. 103

The Indomitable Silence .................................................... 131

Out of My Head ................................................................ 157

Our Farewell ...................................................................... 185

A New Day ........................................................................ 199

Goodbye ............................................................................ 215

# ACKNOWLEDGEMENTS

Creations of love are seldom done alone, and this truth has certainly worked its magic throughout the book you are about to read. Woven into the following pages are many of the beautiful hearts that have touched mine and will do so forever. I wish to thank my wife, Fanny, for her smiles, her joy, and her big heart. My eldest daughter, Chiara, for her playfulness, boldness, and willingness to explore life as a true adventure. My youngest daughter, Alyssa, for her gentle heart, and the music and harmony she brings to our family. You are all gifts from heaven and enrich my life in so many ways, continually inviting me to be the best person I can be. I write these words with a knowing chuckle, as the rewards of family life are often realized through the delicate balance between sweet and tough love.

I was well prepared for this journey by two parents who showed me what it means to walk steadily through life with the sort of strength whose necessary companion is humility. I thank my mum for her never-ending love and selflessness, and my dad for his tireless guidance and wisdom. Together you taught me that the heart's work requires not only benevolence, kindness and compassion, but also intensity, patience and perseverance — indispensable qualities in any project, which my father brought to this book through his relentless hawk's eye for detail.

Finally, I want to thank someone without whom this book would never have come to fruition the way it has. Tom, my friend, I don't

*Acknowledgements*

know how you do it, but somehow you are able to tune into my heart and reveal its unspoken stories. You took over my first lengthy draft and polished it into something that is truly magical. Admittedly, when I saw your first edit it seemed lean, as though limbs were missing. But after my initial shock, the clarity of what you had rendered was apparent and palpable. You had managed to dig deep into my creation and pull it fully into the light, letting it dance in the open space, where I could feel the heartbeat of every word.

When sounds are not in sync, and there is no space in between, they are nothing but noise. But when they are aligned with the heart, they become creations of love. Thank you, Tom! I can hear the music in every page, and I hope you, dear reader, will hear its sounds echo in your heart, too.

# FOREWORD

The smile that remains longer than expected. The warm handshake that feels more than obligatory. The lingering eye contact revealing the willingness to trust. The hug that welcomes you into a world of new friendship. The dream that never leaves you, forever whispering hope through your brightest days and darkest nights. The heart speaks in many ways, and now more than ever we need to listen to its message of love.

We live in an age of growing isolation, as the exigencies of merely existing demand most of our time, attention, and thoughts. And although access to information is literally at our fingertips, it offers us no relief from our loneliness nor clear paths to take, as we grapple with a dizzying array of distractions, short-term answers, and how-to guides. We can find, buy, and research anything without meeting another human being. The online world, despite all its benefits and its plethora of options, cannot guide you through this life. It cannot distinguish what's important to you, worth your time and energy, or essential for your journey.

Leadership and living are becoming more and more urgent and confusing. How do you know you're doing the right things, with the right people, and in the right way? The short answer is you don't — in your head, that is. But that's not where meaningful and lasting connections are ever made. So where, then? A clue is contained in some common daily expressions we often say but rarely ponder:

*Foreword*

*straight from the heart, love with all my heart, know it by heart, give you all of my heart.*

For Angelo Meijers, the answers to the above questions can only be found by first going *into the heart* and seeking our truth in its fierce whisper. There we discover light in the darkness, clarity in the confusion, and serenity amidst the storm. Some may misconstrue this as the quixotic belief that all good comes from good intentions. This would be a mistake, in my view. *The Indomitable Silence* is about the courage to love *while* accepting difficulties, calm in the knowledge that life can be mastered when we're strong enough to embrace who we truly are and reach out with an open and fervent heart.

An experienced business leader and family man, Angelo has seen many problems through to resolution. He is not one to treat challenges lightly. Nor is he one to handle resources wastefully. While the book explores the eternal, to find the love that connects us all, he is aware our time on Earth is limited. So use it well and wisely, he tells us. Apply your time and talent to your heart's work, and you will see not only purpose come into your life, but you will also achieve more meaningful results.

I can speak on this from firsthand experience, for it was in this spirit that *The Indomitable Silence* came to fruition. The premise and purpose of this book manifested in the nature of our editorial collaboration, which beat with an even more robust and unified pulse than we had enjoyed on Angelo's debut publication, *Journey into the Soul*. Let's start at the beginning.

Clear to us from the outset was the deeper our bond, the more cohesive and moving the experience would be, first for us and then for the readers. We had to *feel* the words together or they would fall flat like platitudes, mere lip service to the importance of emotion. So we set out to craft a tale showing just what the heart can accomplish when it speaks the universal language of love and reaches out to

*The Indomitable Silence*

another in search of a shared vision. We embarked on a journey that was bigger than the both of us, and certainly more captivating and transformative than we had expected.

The result was nothing short of thrilling, as we discovered a story far more compelling than we ever could have imagined when we first sat down to discuss this second project. Our creation sang with proof of our premise: that when we let go of our egos and open ourselves to the light of love, the outcome is not only better, it is also the right one. A fantastical new book was born, revealing a world where pathway and destination are inextricably interwoven; where two hearts beat as one, and two souls move in the same direction.

Here we present the product of our pairing. Whereas *Journey into the Soul* soared to the sky and asked who we are as spiritual beings, *The Indomitable Silence* dives deep within, asking how it feels to be a human seeking self-acceptance and connection with others. It is about the magic of the shared experience, its indisputable truth, its unshakable feeling, and its inalienable power to elevate what it means to be fully alive. And it is about the quiet stillness inside, where all things are possible by the grace of eternal love.

Whether you are a business leader, artist, athlete, or any curious soul looking for a deeper, more meaningful connection to yourself and others, we believe this book will inspire you to journey inward, where you can find clarity, truth, and joy, not only in reaching for your potential, but in the profound silence of the smallest of moments. We hope it will help you hear the dreams whispering fiercely in your heart, and that you will carry them out into the world, smiling as you walk through the storm and into the light.

Tom Kernaghan
May 12, 2018

# INTRO

Just like when I wrote my first book, *Journey Into the Soul*, I didn't start this second one with a clear outline, but I have learned from experience that journeys that are perfectly mapped out seldom teach us anything. Nor do they ever turn out as expected. So my approach was to jump in and see where the experience would lead me.

Again I found a book speaking to me, as insights and feelings hidden in the deep chambers of my heart announced readiness to see the daylight. Listen I did. Working for days and sometimes nights, I felt alive with an energy and passion so powerful, I never tired of writing, loving every keystroke and step, no matter how much commitment and patience it required. Clear to me was that I was honoring my gifts and that my heart was ready to share many of its stories, each one opening it up a little bit more.

I could only hope and trust that if I was willing to surrender, to lend all my heart and soul to my hands, then these pages would come alive with a world of words connecting me to you. For that is my task, dear reader, to struggle with the cocooned caterpillar, so that you can join the butterfly as it rises to its fullest flight, on a quest for truth that never ends. This, in my view, is the essence and magic of life; that we transform to our most beautiful true self, and thereby express our greatest potential. Such was the experience I had with a dear old man who shared with me more than words could ever capture.

*Intro*

I remember it all so well. The day was November 12, 2015. Through a mysterious envelope, I was beckoned to a nearby park, where I met him on a lonely bench. Our initial conversation about life's unexpected twists and turns was odd, intense, and deeply moving. The man, who had introduced himself simply as D, spoke with a mysterious blend of tenderness and power that forged an instant heart connection between us. Throughout our encounters that followed, our bond became so strong and familiar that many times I was content to just sit in silence with him and see what unfolded. In fact, it was these moments I have come to cherish the most.

He revealed to me a timeless understanding, and in doing so brought me back to what I had lost: a clear sense of my own heart. D was peaceful, compassionate, and he inspired me to attain a mastery of life he had long since achieved. He was a bright light of love, peace, and humor, and his wisdom went far beyond the borders of conventional understanding and reason. During our times together, he shook the walls I had rebuilt so diligently across the path to my essence. He encouraged me to keep an open mind and never stop questioning my convictions and beliefs, to remain curious about life's mysteries, and to involve my heart and soul completely in whatever I was doing, yet attach to nothing. There was so much to explore, to learn and, maybe most of all, to unlearn. Looking back now, I can see all this was necessary to help me tear down old mental structures and build a new foundation on the pillars of the heart.

Dear reader, as you know best yourself, words have no meaning until they become alive through personal experience and understanding. Each of us is unique, and everything we see, think, and feel depends on our awareness and perspective; there is no right and wrong here. True wisdom arises in a mind not mired in foggy conclusions, but open, spacious, and willing to fly to unknown heights and reach ever higher levels of clarity. However, the path of self-enquiry is not always an easy one. It is much easier to cling to what we think we

*The Indomitable Silence*

know than it is to open ourselves to the possibility that we are only living an illusion we have chosen to believe.

While the mind may lead us along a seemingly safe road, the heart often urges us to take the road less traveled. And it is on this path from the head to the heart where the magic unfolds. There is nothing to lose, for what we leave behind is who we are not, and what is left is the essence of who we truly are — an untarnished jewel of love and light shining in its pure magnificence.

I trust that by going on a journey through this book with me, you will come face to face with your innermost being, and that this experience will continue to live within you long after you have finished the last sentence. Not so much because of the intellectual understanding of what is written, but because the energy contained in the words has fallen into your heart-space, where it casts a light on your own truth and awakens the wisdom of your soul. Embrace the silence and listen to the fierce whisper of your heart. In this sacred stillness, the answers you hear will not be mine, nor anyone else's, but yours only. So keep your mind and heart wide open, and turn the next page. Come with me. The quest is about to begin.

# A LETTER

*I am the silence. I am the silence. I am...*

The words echoed and swirled around me as I opened my eyes and saw the red hand on the clock beside my bed showing 5:10 a.m. Looking to one side, I saw Fanny was already gone. She's an early riser, especially on yoga days, though this degree of eagerness seemed a tad unusual even for her. Otherwise it seemed like a typical morning: the house was quiet, with the girls still asleep, and our dog, Cinnamon, likely downstairs, waiting for his master's return.

As I swung my long legs out of bed and let my feet thud gently on the floor, I reached for my iPhone to check the time again, letting my eyes linger on the date: November 12, 2015. In just over a month it would be our third Christmas in Canada. My wife and the girls were happy, which had brought me a sense of happiness. But my heart still felt out of sync, as if it hadn't fully landed in our new home. In all honesty, I missed the Netherlands: my parents and friends, our old little village, the way of life, and maybe most of all a sense of purpose and belonging. And on that morning two years ago, the cracks were just beginning to show.

My journey to that point had been a varied one, full of challenges and rewards. I had climbed the mountains of childhood shyness and bullying, competitive tennis, and business building. Who would have

*A Letter*

thought I had become what the world calls a "self-made man," living in a breathtaking valley surrounded by so much beauty?

But I knew the only *self* in the equation was in how I had shown up every day. Though I had come a long way from my younger days of self-doubt and found my footing many times, everything I had achieved was with the help, love, and determination of so many who had championed me on my journey. I now longed, probably more than ever, for that sense of connection and purpose. My heart was aching with questions: how do I make a difference as a father and husband, and how can I apply my talents and put my passion to work in this new community? Why, after all the many blessings in my life, do I sometimes still feel so out of tune with my own heart?

As practical as I am spiritual, I put my body in motion. I rose, rubbed my face, and went to the bathroom to get ready for a new day, pondering these questions and anticipating the warmth of my morning coffee and the splendor of our view. As usual, the valley did not disappoint in this respect, as I beheld the landscape while finishing some breakfast. The city lights were dancing like frozen stars on the lake, and in the distance a thin blanket of snow crowned the tops of the green-brown mountains, which would soon be shining under what looked to be a blue-sky morning on the way.

I put on my boots, jacket, and gloves, and stepped outside. Winter was near. Crisp, cool air slapped gently at my cheeks, as though inviting me to go deeper into my contemplative state. Had it been written in my life's blueprint that I would travel to more than fifty countries, see so many different cultures, and meet all these amazing people? Had Fanny and the girls been arranged even before I was born? And what had been my part in all of this, or was it all just fate? It had only been a few months since I had finished the final draft of my first book, *Journey into the Soul.* Michael and Atmos, my two main companions during that part of my journey, had introduced me to a

*The Indomitable Silence*

world where the unfathomable wonder of the universe could exist in a drop of water trickling down your skin.

Still, grappling with the ultimate meaning of those experiences and teachings seemed to have only added to my recent feelings of dislocation and uncertainty. Also, I suspected their full impact was yet to be seen. Also yet to be seen was yesterday's mail, I joked to myself, hoping to alleviate my sense of unrest. We had all been so busy that none of us had bothered to check the postal box.

Taking the long walk to the street, I recalled the many strolls with my dad in my early twenties, during which I would talk hesitantly about what was going on inside, sharing my feelings of confusion and loneliness, eventually finding comfort in our shared space and strength. I thought about *Heal Your Life* by Louse L. Hay, and my amazement at how she cured herself of cancer by using the power of her mind. I remembered my first spiritual teacher who had taught me how to calm the mind and access a place of stillness within I didn't even know existed. In those days, life started to make more sense to me, filled as it was with passion, peace, and purpose. But now, while my life had the shine of worldly success and the appearance of happiness, and though I lived in this beautiful valley, I found myself once again caught up in waves of confusion and doubt. Something had to change.

As I put the key into the box, I felt the first raindrops on my head and saw layers of fog growing denser throughout the valley. Great, I thought, we were getting an inversion, a common weather pattern in the valley during the colder months. The box opened and inside was a blank envelope. Curious, I opened it on the spot and pulled out a short, hand-written letter with the following words: "*I will see you today at 8:30 a.m., near the lake in the city park.*" There was no name, no date, nothing. It was signed with only one letter — a capital D.

*A Letter*

Baffling though it was, this odd little message pushed old thoughts out and posed some new questions to chew on. How could this letter have found its way to the mailbox without even an address on it? Where did it come from? And was it delivered today or yesterday? When I got home, I took off my boots, laid the mysterious note on the kitchen table, and searched my mind for an answer. Nothing came. After my spiritual experiences the summer prior, however, I found myself less leery about stepping into what most would consider a weird or unthinkable situation. Also, quite frankly, I was bored.

Still, the note was strange, and I didn't want to leave my daughters alone. So I waited for Fanny to return and the girls to wake up. After spending some time with them, I decided to give it a go. I jumped into the car and drove over the bridge, into the city. After parking where I often do, I started walking through the park toward the lakeside path. Again I was met with unusual conditions, as the park seemed totally deserted. While the fog was clearing somewhat, I noticed the grounds and benches were all empty except for one. This must be him, I thought. This must be D.

When I was about ten feet away, an older man turned and looked up from behind a scraggly beard and a long, tattered coat. He nodded and grinned, almost imperceptibly. As I drew nearer, I could smell the layers of a rough life his apparent homelessness had laid down upon him. He was shivering, and when I looked into his eyes, I saw many unshed tears straining to burst behind what must have been his last shards of pride.

I sat beside him, thinking of my first experience with Michael the prior summer. How well-groomed he was in contrast to this fellow here! For a few moments we were silently immersed in our inner world, not exchanging a single word. I didn't feel the need to introduce myself, as it would seem redundant after our palpable instant connection. Clearly he was delighted to have someone here who cared, and I was happy just to sit and share my heart with him. I

*The Indomitable Silence*

was enjoying the silence until it occurred to me there wasn't even any morning traffic. Before my mind could address this, he took some pills from a vial and swallowed them in one go. He must have seen the curiosity in my eyes.

Don't worry, these are just painkillers.

I refrained from responding, not wanting to presume too much familiarity. Remembering he had invited me here, I decided to inquire further. "Does it hurt that much?"

Oh, my body has had better days, but I'm all right. And when the pain gets too much, I take a few of these magical buggers.

He then pulled a letter out of his pocket, saying he was allowed to take a certain amount of marihuana for health reasons. Yes, I told myself, I had detected a bit of this aroma.

I know some people look at me with disdain, thinking I'm just one of those homeless druggies, aimlessly wandering around, doing nothing. But I don't give a damn! Compared to many others, I'm still doing reasonably well. I feel blessed to be alive.

Despite the poor condition of his body, I could see a fire burning behind his eyes and sense the passion in the words his heart was speaking. After a few moments of silence, he bowed his head, folded his hands, and the expression on his face turned more serious, even a little dark.

You know, I've lost people I loved dearly and have seen close friends lose everything, even the hope to live another day.

The first tears welled up in the corner of his eyes, and I could tell some of these memories weighed heavily on him.

*A Letter*

It's painful to have no one who wraps an arm around you when you're cold. Someone who makes you feel you're worthy of being loved. Most of my friends didn't die because their body wasn't able to go on; their hearts broke from sheer loneliness and desperation.

A dog suddenly appeared from the other side and started licking his master's legs. The little pooch looked up at me; I smiled at him. By now the man's tears fell abundantly, and his voice broke as he continued.

Do you know what it's like to wake up in the morning with no hope, no joy, and you cannot see the beauty of the sun rising nor hear the sound of the birds singing? To feel no sense of purpose and belonging that gets you through the day, and to fear the moment you close your eyes, afraid of the ghosts haunting your head at night?

He sighed deeply and furrowed his brow, as one particular memory seemed to jab at him.

Can I share a story with you? It's about a long lost friend.

I nodded as he continued, his voice soft and frail, tears still streaming down his face.

His name was Richard, and I had known him for many years. One day he handed me a letter and asked me to read it. But I didn't. I put it aside and told him I wasn't in a hurry. The next day I was wandering in a nearby park, when suddenly a bird's sound caught my attention. I looked up and there he was! His lifeless body hanging in a tree.

He buried his face in his hands and shook. As words could no longer ease the pain, I took his trembling body in my arms. Although I

*The Indomitable Silence*

realized people might walk by any minute, and while I normally would have felt embarrassed, I didn't care now. He needed someone to hold him, to love him.

Since then I've always carried that letter with me. As a reminder that behind someone's eyes there's a life that might be saved by a little love and affection. And that we should never take one day for granted, not even a single moment.

His body was still shaking as he released himself from my arms and searched for something in his left pocket. A crumpled letter appeared. He slowly unfolded it and then read aloud in a trembling voice:

> *My dear friend,*
>
> *I haven't known many people I consider to be true friends. And although I've searched for a long time, I've learned how to live without them. I haven't had the fortune of sharing my heart in the most intimate way, and my wish for children hasn't been granted. Life has not been easy on me. I lost my parents when I was only eight years old. Most of my childhood I spent in orphanages and learned to survive the hard way. It was bully or be bullied; hunt or be hunted. My heart hardened and my mind gradually numbed, first from life and later from alcohol and drugs. Anything to lessen the pain. For years my life carried on, mostly on the streets. I wandered around aimlessly, with a shopping cart as my only loyal companion, searching for something to make life worth living and begging for money to make life possible. The nights were dark and long, but the days were even darker and longer. It's terrible to go through life with no hope, no faith, no purpose.*

*A Letter*

He turned the letter over and continued:

> *But then I met you. I still don't know how in the world you ended up on the streets, because you never shared anything of your past. But to me you were an angel sent by heaven. Through your eyes I saw the goodness in a man's heart, and the beauty of life that had eluded me for so long. Through your friendship I felt safe and knew it was okay to trust someone. Through your heart I felt the warmth and tenderness I thought I had lost. You made me realize that a meaningful life isn't so much about leaving big footprints behind, but the small things we do for each other, just as you have done for me in so many ways. You helped me to regain my faith, not so much because of what you said or some of the books you gave me, but most of all because of the light shining in your eyes and the love working through your hands. You showed me how to appreciate each day as a gift, and that the secret of love is not to ask, but to give; not to take, but to share. Thank you, my dear friend, for all you've given me. I owe you and I'll wait for you, wherever that is.*
>
> *PS: Don't feel guilty. It's my choice. I'm at peace with it.*
>
> *Yours forever, Richard.*

He folded the letter gingerly and put it back in his pocket. He looked upward and gazed into the endless sky, as if to greet his long lost friend.

You know how many times I have asked myself why I didn't read that letter right away? And how many nights I have wailed and beaten my chest out of guilt? Maybe I could have stopped him, or

*The Indomitable Silence*

at least thanked him for the beautiful words and told him how much they meant to me. And wrapped my arms around him one last time. But I didn't.

For a few moments he held his palms open in front of him and moved his lips, as though in silent prayer. Then he lowered his face and turned toward me.

I still don't know why he did it. He was so cheerful, always in for a joke, a helping hand. He was a blessing to be with, such a radiant light. It must have been the pain that was slowly killing him, because in the last year he had been off medication and the other drugs and drink. He wanted to feel his body again, his heart, not be numbed by substances anymore. He was brave. Never heard him complain, not once. He meant the world to me.

He paused and closed his eyes, and I could sense the emotions running through him: the sadness, the pain, the loneliness. I lay my hand upon his, when a sound from above attracted my attention. I looked up and saw a bird sitting on one of the lower branches of a tree nearby. The little fellow was staring at us, and for a moment the thought crossed my mind his old friend had come back to say hello.

I still miss him a lot, and I wish I could turn back the clock.

His eyes opened and landed upon the branch where the bird was singing. The man's face shone with a glow of recognition, and I could feel the melting of his heart. Time stood still as I witnessed a love that merged two worlds into one. Suddenly the bird took off and, as if to say goodbye, made one final circle above our heads before disappearing into the distance. A smile appeared on the man's face, and a twinkle returned to his eyes.

He's in a good place now. The pain has left his body, and his heart. He's free to fly anywhere he wants to go, just like that little bird.

*A Letter*

I know we will meet again. Later, when it's my turn. But for now, there's still something for me to do here.

I thought of my own glimpses of the other side that past summer, and understood what he was referring to. An intensity came over him. He leaned in toward me with a questioning stare.

I would like to read something else he gave me, a couple of months before his farewell letter. Is that okay?

I nodded silently as he took a small note out of the same pocket where he had just put the letter back. Holding the new note and his face upright, he read with a tenderness and strength that was heartwarming to see:

*I don't ask you to hold my pain, I just need you to hold me when I'm hurt.*
*I don't ask you to tell me what to do, I just need you to listen to what troubles me.*
*And I don't ask you to fix me, I just need you to hold space, so my heart can heal.*

*I know you can't take away my pain, for it is mine to bear.*
*I know you can't give me back my self-esteem, for it is mine to restore.*
*And I know you can't solve my problems, for they are mine to sort out.*

*If you can be with me in my lonely hours,*
*listen to what deeply moves me,*
*and hold me in my silent pain.*

*That's when love awakens,*
*and the bird's song in heaven*
*can be heard in our hearts.*

*Richard.*

He bowed his head, as if to give praise to his old buddy. I could sense how much these words meant to him, and to me. "That was beautiful."

*The Indomitable Silence*

He was a poet without an audience. Such a pearl of wisdom and love.

A faint smile marked his face. Something had shifted in him, and in me.

Life has taken me into some deep dark places, as it did for my old friend. And although it was painful and very sad at times, I wouldn't have missed one single day. It shaped me into the person I am today. I'm at peace with who I am, and with my life.

"And happy?"

Happiness has nothing to do with where you are or what you do. It's the essence of who you are! And once you've found that place within, everything you do will have a different quality to it, and everywhere you go will feel very different. Please don't make the same mistake as I did when I looked for happiness in the fleeting experiences of the world: career, wealth, achievements, status, all those things. Turn inward and connect with that pure place beyond pain and pleasure. The part that remains untroubled by strident voices and vexing struggles. That's how you find your joy!

As I listened with growing astonishment to a man who seemed to have found the source of his happiness, I reflected upon my own state of being, of feeling, and had to draw the conclusion that for the most part I was not there yet. Too many times my joy was burdened by the pressures and challenges of daily life. "It seems to me life likes to throw curveballs at us once in a while. Maybe to awaken us, or give us the opportunity to become stronger or more mature. I don't know. But it's definitely not easy to remain calm and peaceful, let alone happy, in this stormy world."

A boat doesn't sink because of the water in the sea, it sinks because of the water that gets in! If your thoughts and feelings

*A Letter*

are determined by forces outside, you'll find yourself floundering in a whirlpool of mental and emotional diarrhea. But once you go beyond this compulsive state and you become more conscious, you can decide what to think and how to feel. Then the mind starts working for you, not against you, now cleaner and calmer. He's a tricky fellow. You'd better make friends with him.

His cute doggie whimpered for some attention, placing a paw on his master's knee. D stroked his head lovingly.

Good boy. My little fellah and your pooch, Cinnamon, not only exist in our minds, that's for sure. Ha! They are as real as can be!

He chuckled and I smiled, not at all concerned about how he knew our dog's name. Not after my recent experiences with my non-physical friends. "Did Michael or Atmos send you?" D's eyes lit up in a momentary flash, and his grin widened.

Not directly, but I do know them! As I can connect to both their world and yours, you might call me a human liaison. When you roam as I do, you get to know people at a glance, and I've seen you many times in the park. That's why I sent you the invitation. Nothing unusual, really.

"Talking about unusual, my life has been very different from what it used to be since we moved into the valley. In the past I have found myself challenged by certain situations, but somehow I always found a way to overcome them, which moved me toward an ever deeper sense of confidence and fulfillment. My tennis, the difficulties in my first jobs, my personal issues, my business… I think all these challenges have made me stronger, more mature. But now? I don't know. It just feels I haven't been my best. And I'm not sure what to do; that's the frustrating part. It's different here, and not only the language." My friend put his hands together and placed his fingertips

*The Indomitable Silence*

to his lips, as he considered his next words very carefully before speaking.

When a flower's seed is planted in the ground, all that's around is dirt, worms, and darkness. But as soon as its head sprouts above the surface, it welcomes the blue sky and the life-nourishing sunlight. The feeling of unfamiliarity can be the sign you're about to flower into something new, something even more beautiful. So, instead of looking down, look up toward the stars and reach for them. You will be filled with renewed hope and enthusiasm, and once that happens, look around and see which other flowers are ready to blossom. When you look through the eyes of the heart, you will know.

I was flabbergasted by the inspiring clarity of his words. Imagining what he must have been through, it touched me deeply that he had moved away so easily from his own pain, to address mine.

You've lost something you loved dearly. That's the emptiness you feel.

I knew he was referring to my business, which had always felt like a baby I had raised to maturity over the fifteen years I had been privileged to walk with her, before I decided it was time to let her go. "It feels like I've lost a child. Not being a part of her journey still hurts sometimes."

A child never leaves a mother's heart. True love never dies. Don't be too hard on yourself. You can't push her out.

"But it's over, and I don't want to feel this emptiness anymore. It's time to move on!"

Well, you're talking to me here on a park bench! So, clearly you're still on a quest.

*A Letter*

My first impression of him as a helpless, homeless old man had evaporated like snow in the sun by now. He seemed to know a lot about me, my life, and the aching beat of my heart. I decided to tap into his wisdom. "And where does this quest take me?" D just smiled.

To yourself, of course. Into your heart. And then into the world.

In an instant the atmosphere around us changed. A sudden breeze blew the remaining fog up into a swirl, and I saw the morning sun shimmering on the lake and dappling the mountains beyond. Sounds of people in the park and the city behind us came to life. I asked him if he never felt lonely, and again his eyes lit up like diamonds in the dark.

Loneliness is not determined by the number of people you are with, but by the amount of treasures you keep within. When the soul hears music but you refrain from singing, or when the heart burns with passion but you're too afraid to act on it, that is loneliness. And in moments where I do feel alone, I still have my little companion here.

Glider looked up at him and squinted with expectant affection. D returned his love with an affectionate scratch of his wiry-haired head. The pooch placed his head back down to continue sleeping.

Not everything has worked out the way I planned or expected, and I have made many mistakes along the way, many poor judgements. I have hurt people and failed my words many times. But there's one thing I have no regrets about. I have lived! I have tasted the flavor of life in all its sweetness and bitterness, all its confusion and wonder.

"Don't you miss any of the stuff you once had? Answer truthfully now." He grinned at my playfulness.

*The Indomitable Silence*

As long as you don't feel at home within yourself, in your heart, nothing feels like home. You can be in the most beautiful place, and yet all the comfort and convenience won't bring you a sense of belonging, of purpose. I don't think anything in this world is truly ours. We've only been given the opportunity to use and enjoy all of this as long as it takes. I consider it a loan life has given us. Only this one doesn't need to be paid back.

"Ha!" Glider started, looked up at me, and sniffed my leg; I patted him. "Nice analogy."

We're all passengers in time. Our home, our car, our money, all change hands at some point in time. Even our children.

I sensed a sudden sadness in his voice, as he continued flipping through the book of life.

Life is too short to waste our precious time. I've emptied myself of all that doesn't matter, so that what truly matters could reveal itself. That's why I can see who I truly am.

"I always thought it takes a lot of time, self-reflection, and spiritual practice, to come to know oneself."

You don't need to learn who you are, you only need to unlearn who you are not! Find the source of life in your heart and the rest will be given to you. But remember, the heart nests where the head wanders and the hands serve. So your thoughts and actions do matter. It's just that you no longer need to do anything to become something. You are already whole in your essence! And once you realize this and, even more importantly, feel it, all you think and do will have a different perfume about it.

He stood up, a bit shakily, and Glider rose by his side. I moved to help him, but he waved me off with a gentle thank you. I kept a watchful eye on him. "I envy you. You have nothing, yet you seem to have everything a human heart longs for. And I have so much, yet my heart still feels empty at times, restless." He shuffled along for a few steps before getting a more sure footing, and then looked out over the water.

Waves rise and fall, both in your head and heart. Don't try to fight them, or even calm them. You cannot. The waves are the result of the energy built up inside, combined with the energy gathered by others who sail on the same ocean. But what you can do is dive beneath the turbulence of the waves and experience a world of serenity and beauty, one even I have only begun to comprehend. And I am near the end of my life!

"The source is the water itself. I remember this from Michael. That's who we are!" I felt my chest tighten with a surge of conviction that surprised me, as it did D. He looked over his shoulder at me. He also appeared pleased by this sudden reappearance of my passion.

Look back at your life, all that you've overcome and achieved. When it counted, was it ever a wave, or something deeper inside of you? Your heart and your truth, my friend. What do you think you're doing as a father and husband?

"That's with all my heart, I hope."

And do you think your children care about your fancy accomplishments and trophies? Or any of your contemplations and insecurities?

"Ha ha! I most certainly know they do not!" His face took on a wistful, faraway look, as he recalled a time clearly held dear to him, and his eyes began to water.

Neither did mine. Neither did mine.

*The Indomitable Silence*

He turned away, crying gently. I was curious but gave him a moment, during which I could hear some other park-goers behind us, talking, laughing. The morning was beginning to warm up. "I'm so sorry."

These emotions hurt when they pass through me. But I no longer add another layer by telling myself it shouldn't have been this way, or what I might have done better. The waking mind plays tricks. I've come to trust my dreams much more.

"Ah dreams … aren't they just another perspective of reality? Life's way of showing us a world that lives within, teaching us what we may have overlooked or shied away from? My spiritual friends taught me that this past summer." D turned to me again, looking more composed than before.

Maybe we're even more awake at night than during daytime. I don't — ouch!

His reaction had escaped him before I could see the impact of a Frisbee, which now fell by his feet as he rubbed his forehead. Glider barked. A surge of protective energy arose in me as I bolted upright and glared around. "Hey! Who threw that?! Watch what you're doing!" A young man bounded toward us, looking apologetic while at the same time trying not to grin as his friends taunted him. Glider growled, but D calmed him with the easy skill of a longtime master.

Thank you, but it's okay. A man alone rather enjoys his moments with others. Life and Frisbees happen without warning, as you can see!

The young man expressed his regrets as I handed him his toy. He sprinted back to his buddies, and D and I looked at each other. Soon we found ourselves smiling, then chuckling, and then laughing out loud like teenagers ourselves. "I guess this world is real enough in some ways!" And we laughed some more. Glider barked, wanting

*A Letter*

to be included. We three returned to the bench and sat, catching our breath. Soon D became contemplative again.

The universe is a strange and funny place.

"And friendly?" The moment those words left my mouth, I already felt bad. Here I was with a man who had certainly not been treated very gently by life, and I was talking about a friendly universe. What was I thinking?!

I don't know. It looks friendly when something nice happens, but it can also be quite a challenging place. Physically. Just ask an astronaut!

I was glad he hadn't taken the question too personally. "I'm sorry. That was a stupid question."

No, it's not. You want to understand the nature of life, so you need to question, explore, and investigate everything. That's all fine. But don't forget that God laughs at our thoughts ... and our plans.

"Why do you say that?"

Oh, nothing. It's just that some people think they can create anything they want in this universe. Only in their minds. Manifesting their desires, that kind of thing. But a flower doesn't grow because you want it to. It needs the right conditions and the right care. And so do you, to grow in light and love. This is how you and the universe evolve. No amount of desire, expectation, or belief, will work if you don't do the right things. Surely you've learned this to get to where you are now.

I reflected on this point, remembering the hours upon hours of diligent work combined with the desire to succeed, in tennis and in business, and how in the end none of these endeavors could completely fulfill

*The Indomitable Silence*

my heart. Clearly something more was waiting. "So what were you putting out into the universe that brought that Frisbee?" D shot me a sideways glance.

Maybe the same energy with which you now ask that smart-ass question!

"Ha ha. Sorry, it's in my nature."

Don't be sorry. Humor is part of God's nature as well. You think creating a universe would be possible if the work were always a downer? My gosh!

"Do you think there's a childlike playfulness and benevolence to this universe?"

Who cares? Even if I say yes, what does it do for you? Are you more happy, more peaceful? No! Listen, the only thing that matters is your own experience, how you feel inside. Don't try to understand life intellectually, instead enter it, live it, and play in it — like a sandbox in your house!

"Like the father in that movie *Close Encounters of the Third Kind*?"

Ha! An entertaining comparison.

"His family and neighbors thought he'd lost it."

Until it was clear he had found the truth. Besides, do you really care what people say? I can tell you don't. But I can also tell that—

"I do care what my family thinks!" He had struck a sensitive chord here.

*A Letter*

Then show them your heart. There's nothing that compares to the feeling of being loved. Don't ever take that for granted! I wish I still had my loved ones with me.

My heart's desire to see my family happy mingled with a profound sadness that was passing through D. I sensed he was about to share something very personal. A deep feeling of dread gripped my chest as he looked into the distance, glassy-eyed. "Oh dear… You lost your…?"

First my parents, and later my wife and children. My parents showed me what true love is. They were a wonderful example of a harmonious marriage, and I feel blessed I was their son. They died a natural death and I'm grateful they didn't need to suffer a lot nor miss each other for too long. Dad passed away pretty soon after Mum, and I'm sure she was already waiting for him. Their death wasn't hard to accept, but losing my wife and especially my little angels was quite a different story.

"What happened? If I'm not intruding…"

They died more than ten years ago. An accident on the road that … yeah…

"I'm so sorry."

I have learned to live without them, but life has never been the same since. They say time heals all wounds, but the heart is beyond time. It still feels like yesterday.

His voice broke when he spoke these last words, and I could feel his heart opening up even more and the love for his family flowing out. I put my hand on his shoulder. He continued.

The day they died, a part of me died with them. Many nights I cried myself to sleep, wishing I could kiss them one more time. And when

*The Indomitable Silence*

I woke up, the first thing I did was to wish them good morning, as if they were still with me. Nobody should have to bury their own children.

By now I had a hard time controlling my emotions, too, but I tried to hold back out of respect for his sadness. "I cannot even imagine what you've been through."

Many lonely times I screamed "why?" to God, even cursing Him. But all I heard back was this deafening silence ... and my tormenting thoughts. What did I really know about life, about the soul's journey and why they had to leave this soon?

I recalled what I had learned from Michael and Atmos, that souls make contracts in the other realm, including possibly the moment of death, though I thought it best not to mention. D must have heard what was going through my mind.

Yes, I want to believe there's a reason why life took them so quickly away from me. But it's nevertheless hard. Who knows why these things happen? By the way, never feel you have to block your emotions around me. I can take it.

"Okay, I'll try to remember that." I was intrigued he was already planning future conversations between us.

But what I do know is they are still with me, my sweet angels. Sometimes I can feel them just a whisper away.

"You said true love never dies. And I think you're right."

All that seemed so important became unimportant the day they died: career, goals, desires, worries, fears. Death had taken them all into its grave. But death also opened my eyes to the real values in life: the hearts we touch, the light we carry, the laughter and tears we share. But it's not easy, it's...

*A Letter*

His emotions had become too much, and I knew it wasn't the time for hollow words. I wrapped my arm around his now hunched shoulders, and felt the quaking of his grief.

Losing my wife felt not as hard as losing my kids. I can still see her. Her joyful heart, her wonderful smile that brought laughter and light to so many. Thank you for being with me here.

We sat for some time without speaking. My heart tried to capture the intimacy of the moment, as I knew it would end. A hush returned to the park as people wandered off to their days. Eventually his voice broke the silence.

I have chosen to cherish their lives over the grief of their death. When I think about them, I want to smile, not cry. I want to remember the good times, not dwell in the loss and sadness. But I will tell you, passing through the door to your heart is a tough journey when it's not wide open. The good news is you don't have to travel to that door alone. Focus on me!

His mood had changed again in the blink of an eye, as I watched him lay his hand upon his chest and close his eyes. Hesitant at first, I did the same. To my astonishment, I could still see him — or rather, us — as though I were hovering around, out of my body.

Have you ever wondered why we close our eyes when a sweet memory comes to mind? Or when we kiss, pray, or listen to our favorite music? It's because the most beautiful moments cannot be seen by the eyes, only felt in the heart. That's where beauty resides. Then you awaken, and...

I opened my eyes and his voice drifted off. My body felt like it had been hit by lightning, yet strangely I was calm and peaceful inside. Though my future was still unknown to me, and my choices were yet

*The Indomitable Silence*

to be made, I knew I wanted to feel this way every day. I just had to find my way through that door he mentioned.

Just be grateful you are alive, for each moment bears the opportunity to bring light, to be that light!

"You thanked me for being here, but I'm the one who's glad *you* are here."

Love is all we need, my friend. Even on this park bench on a cold November morning.

Glider jumped up on my leg to play with me. Smiling, I picked him up and scratched his little head. My heart was overcome by joy as a pocket of warm air pushed the cool away and surrounded us on the bench. Then, to my astonishment, the space between us gave way to a soft green glow that embraced all three of us. Before curiosity and confusion could take hold of me, D told me to look at him. I raised my head, the rest of the park disappeared, and then we were gone…

# THE CABIN

I found myself walking up the steep mountain across the lake, on a rocky path with some of the most spectacular vistas in the valley along the way. As drizzling rain dampened my hair, I wondered how I could be up here so quickly, in a place that takes 20 minutes by car. Looking for logic and my lungs heaving with exertion, I jerked with a start when a voice broke the sound of my breathing.

Hello!

My heart skipped a few beats. There he was, smiling reassuringly like someone I had known for years. Dressed in a brown suede jacket, blue jeans, black belt, and brown boots. Around his neck a silver cross attached to a thin leather cord hung loosely over a white T-shirt. He looked like he had walked straight out of a remake of a seventies road trip movie. Only now, as he approached, I noticed he was clean shaven.

You look surprised.

"Is that really you?"

Of course, who else?

"But—"

How could I make it here so quickly?

*The Cabin*

"Well, yes."

Have you forgotten about your travels through time and space with your soul-buddies this past summer? Here, give me a hand.

We had come to a narrow, steep climb that I thought would be a hard scramble for D on his own. He reached out his hands, and with a gentle pull I helped him over the rocky hump. I couldn't help but notice he looked younger and healthier than in the park, though I knew enough not to be baffled by this. Still, I couldn't help myself. "But I thought you were just a *liaison*."

Ah, well I was speaking figuratively. But I do pick up some of the tricks from the spiritual realm. I must, if I am to ... liaise. Ha ha. Besides, if we never reach beyond our current grasp, we would still be warming ourselves by fire alone and crossing continents on horseback.

I looked more closely at him and noticed not only his hair but also his clothes were completely dry, whereas I was getting soaked through. "Right now I feel like a cat that's fallen into a bathtub!" D let out a roar of laughter, which was followed by a loud woof and bark. I turned to see Glider scampering up the stones behind us. He first jumped against my legs before going on to his master, who bent down and tousled his fur affectionately.

Oooh, hello there! See, does little Glider here not seem real to you? He smells like a wet dog to me. You two have that in common. Ha! You could say it's raining ON cool cats and dogs here.

He smiled at his own cheesy quip, as my thoughts turned to Cinnamon and his playful nature, and I wondered how my girls' day was going.

You're thinking about your family.

*The Indomitable Silence*

"Yes, how do you know?" Even as I asked this, I realized it was a silly question given all that was happening. But I persisted. "Do your friends on the other side teach you the trick of reading minds?" He shot me a serious look, and his intense blue eyes mesmerized me. He looked quite different from before, and yet some ineffable essence remained the same.

No, life on this side has taught me how to read hearts. And yours is still troubled, as is your mind about who I am and how I look this way.

"One more mystery in a sea of mysteries!"

Ah, people and their need for mastery over mystery. The other way around is so much more fun. Let's keep going.

We walked in silence for a while, only the sound of wet stones crunching underfoot. I looked around at the lay of the land. "This trail is near our house, I think. But I've never hiked this far up the mountain."

Yes, it is. But right now you're on a journey to a different kind of home. And as for who I am, just think of me as an old friend who has walked the passage of time a little longer than you have.

"I don't even know why I'm here."

You need me. And, to be honest, I also need you.

"I see..."

Not yet, but you will. I have something to teach you, which you can share with others.

"Share with others ... how?"

*The Cabin*

Another book! I've read your first one. Fascinating! Journey into the Soul...

"But—"

You're seriously going to question this after we just teleported across the lake in the snap of a finger? Yes, I know the book isn't out yet. But it will be. And you got a lot of the basics right. The spiritual stuff, I mean.

"Hey, it's *my* quest, so there *is* no right!" He bowed toward me slightly, grinning.

Right you are. I was just testing you. And the second one will be how it feels to be in your heart. I'm here to help with that. You'll find me a little less wordy than your friend Michael, though. Atmos is cool. He says little.

"Well, I hope the heart knows enough to grasp what I'm reaching for. The first book is ambitious, I think. We shall see..."

It's wonderful to aim high and reach out for the stars. But never forget to take someone with you. The view is better when at least two hearts behold it.

"High winds blow on high hills, so I'm always cautious when speaking about my ambitions and deepest desires. I might disappoint myself, or others. Or my ideas might seem a bit unusual, even whacky."

So? Who remembers the green turtles, when you can dream of the blue ones?

"Ha, I remember that Sting album *The Dream of the Blue Turtles*! Love it. Still play it once in a while. But I take your meaning: a new beginning. I want to speak my truth, share what's in my heart."

*The Indomitable Silence*

There's a reason you feel this nudge inside. Lead yourself with it first, to your highest potential. And when you're up there, share what you see and feel. You would be surprised how many hearts are waiting to open and connect. Come, let's keep walking. I'll tell you a story.

We began moving up an incline, and I hung back a step just in case he would stumble. I noticed the rain had eased and the clouds were beginning to part. The weather vagaries of the valley! Glider moved alongside, panting contentedly. I was surprised and amazed at how well D handled himself, as he seemed to have found renewed vigor on this path, which was clearly familiar to him. Without taking his eyes off the trail, he began.

Once there was a man who spent most of his days contemplating the meaning of life. He searched his mind, his possessions, his highly acclaimed status, but none of these could give him a sense of lasting fulfillment and contentment. He went to church and tried to find the answer in the stories about a heavenly Father, but even faith didn't give him what his heart was looking for. He wasn't in fact unhappy, for he had a wonderful wife, lovely children, and a successful career, but somehow there was this emptiness still lingering inside.

Then one day he became seriously ill, and the reality hit him that tomorrow might never come. He felt sad for the hearts he hadn't touched and the talents he hadn't used. He realized he had mainly lived in his head, using the present moment as a means to get somewhere, instead of enjoying the fullness of the Now. That day his life changed forever, and he was on his way to his heart.

"What happened next? Was he okay?"

I don't know. I lost sight of him.

*The Cabin*

"Then how can you tell his life would never be the same?"

Because when the heart expands, it never returns to its previous state.

"I guess that's why I acted on a silly letter in my mailbox!" From behind I could see D's cheeks rise, and I knew he was cracking a wide smile. He stayed quiet as I continued. "You're one of a kind. I've never met someone like you, who seems to come up with all the right answers." I found him fascinating, and his staggering ability to go from such sorrow to such levity within one morning blew me away, and the thought of it now put wings on my feet as we walked ever higher.

You also know the answers, deep in your core. Just ask the right questions. And keep walking.

"Walking higher to go deeper! Nice."

Life is a paradox, as you've probably noticed. And the art of living is not to put everything into the seed of logic, but to ride its contradictions. There are no guarantees, nor free rides. But there is a path to inner stillness and clarity. There is a path—

"And you will help me find it."

Actually, you're on it right now. I was being literal as well. Ha ha. We're going to my place, remember?

"Oh, I had already forgotten about that. Too lost in my head."

I can show you a way out. The mind is like a parachute, it only works when it opens up. Then you can fall gently out—

"Of my mental cobwebs—"

*The Indomitable Silence*

Into your heart! Softest landing there is, and the cleanest one, too. When you're completely involved in what you do, fully open without holding back, life touches you in ways unimaginable. Say, did you ever return a serve from the stands when you played tennis?

"No, of course I didn't. But I'm sure there were some spectators who thought they could take me, especially on my bad days."

And I'll bet when you played with all your heart, you connected more closely with the spectators and fans.

"You're right. But that was a long time ago. My concern today is my family and future, and protecting the love we share."

Let me ask you a question. When you are in love, can anything get to you?

"Well, that's been quite a while. Ha ha. But I see where you're going with this. No, of course not. It feels like you can walk on water."

Because the energy is so strong you simply rise into it. Now tap into that feeling. And don't be afraid, because anything other than love won't find any hook to hold onto. I know Michael must have taught you this.

We continued our walk, feeling the bliss of the quiet, hearing every rock and twig crunching underfoot, and enjoying the gentle panting of Glider. His last words took me back to my visits with Michael only months earlier, and I wondered if he could see me now. I didn't want to forsake the wisdom he had given me. So I didn't fight back with thoughts, as I'm often inclined to do. I surrendered. D must have sensed this change in me. He continued.

The path is to return to your original state of pureness, of innocence. Therefore you must not run away from the darkness,

35

*The Cabin*

or build walls around the heart, but bring it back into the light. Then it becomes the light!

Just then he swung his arm back toward me, and without thinking I raised my arms and parried the blow. Though older, he was stronger than expected. I glared at him in indignant shock as I regained my footing. "What the hell was that?!"

See! You'll always protect what needs protecting. But in matters of the heart, that which you hold onto holds onto you. So let everything flow through you, without any obstruction. Whatever needs to stay will stay, and whatever is not needed will leave. Allow life to touch you, to embrace you, and —

"Stay open!"

Yes. Remember your girls as babies and how they were open to their ever-changing emotions. Or look at Glider here, or your own pooch. No emotional or mental stuff gets stuck to them. They live in the moment; they let it flow. That's how the heart stays open. We're almost there.

"We'll see. I have some more work to do, I think."

No, I was being literal again. Ha ha. We're getting closer to my little palace.

"Oh! So your palace—"

Is just up ahead. Sometimes you get what you want, other times not. Don't be driven by that dynamic, or it will close down the heart. And don't blow up your ego, your self-importance, for it will become so heavy that it will crush the heart. Not making it about you will make you happier. Funny, hey? This is one of life's most delicious paradoxes.

*The Indomitable Silence*

"Speaking of delicious, do you happen to have any food. Um … I assume you have a kitchen?" He looked back at me with his eyebrows raised. I gave him a small grin and shrugged. "I know that's rude, but…"

Well, "Ask, and it will be given," as the Bible says. Why not include snacks in that? Nice to see you still have your athletic reflexes, by the way.

"Gee, thanks for confirming my muscle memory!" Without breaking stride, D smirked and reached down to scratch Glider's head and ears. The little dog looked up and squinted at him contentedly. "Any more advice?"

Welcome everything that comes your way with a smile, as if you had chosen it. Always say yes to the present moment, but dare to say no when someone tries to screw you.

"Oh, I've said a lot of noes in my life."

Maybe not often enough?

D looked at me, and our eyes met in mutual understanding. He was right. I had been naive a few times too many, in business, in money-matters, in friendships. I had trusted people when I shouldn't have. Feeling hot and perturbed by these unwanted memories, I changed the topic."Gee, where is that place of yours?! Saying yes to the present moment is easier if you know where you're going," I quipped. "And if you don't get so damn tired!"

I winked at D as he smiled and angled his head up the trail toward an open space. We had to avoid some old, fallen trees and a small pile of rocks. Despite his age, he moved nimbly, with ease and grace. Even little jumps were more of a hindrance to me than to him. Then, as we cleared the hurdles, I looked out on a small meadow overlooking

*The Cabin*

the frosty mountain expanse and the sun-dappled lake below. It was stunning, even in November. "Wow, that is something!"

Amazing, isn't it? Just a few steps and a change of perspective unfolds. Beauty is all around, as you can see. Feel free to take a picture, mijn vriend.

I turned my head and our eyes met. He had spoken in my native Dutch! D put an arm around me, and I felt a warm swell in my chest. He smiled broadly, as a parent might on seeing his child's joy on Christmas morning.

I heard your accent. Hey, you don't get to my age without picking bits of other languages. I didn't say the mind wasn't good for some things. But it can only see so much. Come, let's go.

We walked through the meadow awhile, enjoying the sun through the broken clouds, when D turned to me just as something amazing happened: a ray of sunlight turned from yellow to warm green, revealing what appeared to be a small structure tucked behind a rocky outcrop up ahead. Glider looked up at his master, who with a slight nod of permission sent the little dog running with unbounded enthusiasm toward a little wooden shack now coming into full view. Without questioning the change in atmosphere, I followed D to the front deck.

Welcome to my humble cabin in the sky.

I could tell he was proud, but not in an arrogant way. He took a deep breath, and I took it all in. Though it was simple and crude, the cabin looked surprisingly sound and strong, much like the man himself — at least up here on the mountain. "You built this yourself?" I could hear the amazement and mild disbelief in my voice. So could he.

*The Indomitable Silence*

Yes, I know, how does a man like me build this place way up here? With my own hands, over what felt like a lifetime. Come on in. Glider, buddy, you stay out here and guard us.

Glider settled by his food and water bowl next to the door. D pushed his rough thumb on the door handle and opened the latch with a *clack* so sharp and pronounced that the sound seemed to fill the entire valley. The rough scuff of our boots on the wooden porch gave way to the contained shuffling of two grown men in a small space. And yet it didn't feel cramped, as it was clean and bright in its minimalistic decor: a modest kitchenette on one side, a wooden table, a couple of chairs, a small bed tucked in one corner, and windows on each of the four walls. Except for a mirror, a burning oil lamp, and a few photo albums, there was not much else. Just a small, painted chest at the foot of the bed. He moved toward it, pointing to the table and chairs.

Please, have a seat.

I did so, as he bent over the trunk and took out a pad of lined paper and a pen. He tossed it on the table and then made his way over to a wood stove I would have expected in a cottage generations ago. Crouching, he opened its front door and got a fire going with such impressive speed and skill that I could barely see his hands moving. He stood up and put the kettle on. I looked at the far corner and noticed a few water jugs, most of them filled. Clearly, he was off the city grid.

Cream and sugar, I assume.

"Yes, please. I shouldn't be surprised that you know how I take my coffee." With the same swiftness, he prepared two mugs, squatted, and opened a compartment beneath the floor, from which he pulled out some cream and sugar, along with some packaged cupcakes. He smiled at my curious expression.

*The Cabin*

You would be amazed at what the earth keeps cool for us. Not to mention a double-lined container with saw dust in between its walls. Do all this and you have a good, old-fashioned "ice box." And the paper and pen are for you, when you're ready.

Soon the coffee was ready, and mugs and cupcakes were on the table. Pulling a chair out roughly, he sat across from me with his feet splayed out, his face warm and welcoming. We sipped quietly. I wanted to laugh at the oddness of how this day was unfolding, all from a tiny decision to check for the mail first thing in the morning. And yet somehow that move felt like the distant past. I gazed at him over my coffee as he studied my face.

How do I live here, you wonder? Well, I set myself small tasks every day to use my body and mind, so that I don't get old too soon. I read, cook, garden... I even do some writing. A man can live without means, my friend, but not without meaning.

"Clever." I paused and took a sip from my mug. "I think this simple piece of wisdom applies to the new generation, at least in the more affluent parts of the world. Among youngsters these days, there's a lot of boredom, depression, even suicides. They can see the whole world pass by on their smartphones, but many lack passion in their hearts. Plenty of friends on social media, but so few when the shit gets heavy. Surrounded by peers, yet driven by fears. Drinking and drugs make for poor friendships."

They will learn, though. You can support them, tell them what you think, but they have the right to make their own choices.

"And mistakes."

What you think is right doesn't have to be the right thing for somebody else. Don't get caught up in self-righteousness. There's already enough of that. Ha! Just ask your children.

*The Indomitable Silence*

"Talking about our children, what's the most important thing we can give them?"

You don't need to give them anything, except for some new clothes now and then. Girls, you know...

"Very funny, but I'm serious. What did *you* give your children? There must have been something."

Man, you don't give up, do you?

"Not easily, no. It's one of the things I teach my kids."

Teaching is one thing, showing is another. Children don't so much listen to your audio, they watch your video. So be the change you want to see in your kids. They will remember. That's more than enough.

"Could you give me a little more of the audio, please?"

Okay, if you really want to know... Feed their hearts with love, not fear. Fill their minds with gratitude, not greed. And show them the wonder of life, not only the price of things. Now please, let an old man enjoy his well-deserved coffee while it's still hot.

I let my questions run dry, for the moment, and we both sipped in silence. As I put the mug down and collected my thoughts, I noticed him glancing sideways, directing my eyes to something in a section of the cabin I hadn't looked at too closely. And there were the words, the same ones that had echoed in my mind earlier that morning. Here they were stencilled on a mounted piece of wood: *I am the silence.* I felt a shot of invigorating cool run through me, as though someone had opened doors in my body to let the breeze in. D just watched me. "Oh, those words—"

*The Cabin*

Are just a beginning. People often make it too big, too intellectual, when they talk about the grand purpose of life. Even Michael and Atmos didn't show you the full arc of your story here on Earth. You must live each scene of your movie moment by moment. Eventually the bigger picture will reveal itself.

"What picture has revealed itself to you?"

Like you, I used to be driven, racing around, chasing success. I enjoyed it most of the time, though, for what it was worth. But in the end it never brought more meaning to my waking hours. I yearned for something deeper. Now I value the joy of having little. I've stopped searching for the life I want and asking for more; instead I'm grateful for the life I've been given.

"Going with the flow, as the saying goes." He saw me eyeing the cupcakes and motioned with his hand for me to help myself. I selected one with the chocolate sprinkles, as it reminded me of *hagelslag* back in the Netherlands. Before biting in, I said, "I miss my old home sometimes. It was smaller than my current one, but cozy. Lots of beautiful memories are still there. Now, I'm not sure where the flow is taking me."

Many change their landscape when they feel lost. Change work, homes, even partners, all in order to find a sense of purpose, of belonging. But this crazy, noisy world offers no perfect place to go, or to hide. Home is right underneath your nose, but you don't see it if you stare too far in the distance, however beautiful the view may be.

As I looked out at the valley and lake below, D stood up and opened all the windows with such alarming speed and force that the cabin seemed to shake. Although it couldn't have been more than a few degrees outside, the fall breeze that rushed in was not cold but warm and embracing. He sat down again and opened his long arms, as if

*The Indomitable Silence*

to say anything was possible and everything would be okay. D then grinned and nodded at the pad and paper to my left.

Drop those words right here.

Though I wasn't exactly in the mood to write, I reached for the paper and pen. I rolled the latter between my thumb and index finger, feeling its power to serve my expression. I looked at him, at the saying on the wall, and wrote: "*I am the silence...*" I put the pen down. We smiled and continued with our coffees, without speaking for a while. "You told me this morning that you don't give a damn what people think of you. But what gives them the right to judge you?"

What others think is none of my business! And most people don't even really know me, so who cares? Listen, if you can fully accept every aspect of yourself, you won't be sensitive to judgment. Nor will you feel the need to judge. I think it's not so much people's words that hurt but your own wounds, your lack of self-acceptance.

"I'm not too sure about that."

Words can never hurt.

"Oh, sure they can."

No! Words can only touch what's already hurting inside. When I was a young adult, I tried to please people, and the more I did, the more I became a stranger to myself. This went on until I realized the only person I should please is myself, by being true to who I am. The world can see you as a success, but if you see yourself as a failure, you'll feel like one. Now, that is sad.

I had to admit he was right on this point, as I remembered the days way back in time when I didn't feel so good about myself. In fact I didn't like myself at all, while I was still very successful as a young tennis player.

*The Cabin*

It's not the applause that makes the heart sing, it's how you feel inside. Whatever you need and aren't willing to give to yourself, you start looking for in others. If you can't forgive yourself, you need forgiveness from others. If you don't praise yourself for a job well done, you need others to praise you. If your heart is closed, you need...

"I suppose you're right." I watched him as he took another sip, tilted his head, and squinted.

Tell me what happened when you first met your wife.

His sudden change of subject was a bit strange, again, but I decided to go along with it. "Oh! Well..." I sat back in my chair, relaxed, and fell into a daydream. "I was in a discotheque in Bandung, Indonesia, about twenty years ago. The music was playing, the lights were swirling, and she was so beautiful. I immediately knew she was the one." He smiled as though he knew the story already and was just indulging me.

Ah, the irresistible energy of love and passion. Boom! Your eyes met, your hearts were on fire, and all you wanted was to be together. Two hearts had become one! I know the feeling.

"*Two hearts had become one.* That's certainly how it felt! But, like with most intimate relationships, we've struggled at times to keep that closeness." I paused and sipped my coffee, to gather myself, as D waited calmly. "I don't want to lose what I have. I want to make sure I'm doing the right things." I felt a vague sadness and tightness in my chest. D leaned forward, grabbed one of my hands, and looked me straight in the eyes.

Love is the only thing that multiplies when you share it. Don't ever forget that. Being afraid to lose what you have will do no good. You have to open up and give from the heart; that's what those

44

*The Indomitable Silence*

around you will feel. And that's how love will find its way back to you.

"It seems to me most people are more focused on getting more money, stuff, and recognition, than love." D sat back up, a little angrily, and I could tell this topic was deeply important to him. I sensed a rant was coming, and I was right about that. He leaned against the table again.

I was talking about you, brother! But you're right, there's an emotional and spiritual vacuum these days. So many divorces, lonely hearts, fear and anger. And why? Just because someone else has a little bit more?! I'm asking you, more of what? Everyone seems to be running a rat race without knowing what they're pursuing, or even why!

He took a short breather to gather his thoughts. Then he went on.

Success seems to be solely determined by the amount of money we make, so we can buy all these fancy things we don't even need. And we get so absorbed in our jobs that we don't have, or take, the time to really connect with those around us. In our social isolation we get sick from loneliness, and then turn to prescription drugs, addictions and distractions to escape the pain. It's absurd! Do you know what I would give to share just THIS day with my family, if they were here?! THAT is loss, my friend! That is...

He sat back, and I could feel the anger and pain passing through. The breeze picked up, ruffling the pad of paper and pushing the pen a few inches. I closed the cupcake package. D took a few deep breaths and began to calm down.

Why can't we just share the good things of life with one another and keep the bad things to ourselves? Sharing the bad stuff and protecting the good stuff is not the way to harmony in the world, nor in our hearts. Have another cupcake, by the way.

*The Cabin*

"Oh, thanks. They're good!" I opened the pack and this time took a caramel one.

We need to take care of each other, because when others hurt, we hurt. And when we blossom, others blossom. We cannot only think about ourselves, shut our eyes, and believe the world will be fine. It won't. We are the world! Enjoy the treat you're eating, by all means.

He smiled with teasing good nature, and I welcomed the lighter mood. We laughed and then sat in silence for a while, enjoying the breeze moving steadily throughout the cabin. A slight whimper and low growl came through the door, and I looked over my shoulder.

Glider makes those noises when he's dreaming.

I could see the happiness on D's face at the thought of his little canine companion. Clearly he wasn't done, as he continued giving me some extra pieces to the puzzle.

Give what you would love to receive. Give of your time, your energy, your talents, and the resources at your disposal. But do so out of love, because of what's close to your heart, not to rid yourself of guilt or serve only your interests. Giving isn't an obligation, but a privilege you're granted. A gift, a connection with others that can stay inside them forever, for them to pass on. Go within... Go within... Go within...

Before I could wrap my mind around his weird repetition, the atmosphere inside the cabin became perfectly still. His eyes penetrated mine once more, finding their way into an inner world that now seemed to appear real all around us. D's presence dissolved behind a growing violet and blue light, which swirled around the table before casting a hologram-like stream of images from my life: my wife and two daughters, the places we had lived and traveled,

*The Indomitable Silence*

my parents. I looked up at D and saw how his eyes were moist with emotion. Then the succession of familiar scenes gave way to a scene I did not recognize…

*I was lying on a patch of roadside grass one evening in our former hometown in the Netherlands. It was warm and it felt like summertime. The sun was about to set and a myriad of dancing lights colored the sky. My youngest, Alyssa, was beside me, and our bikes were nearby. It struck me that she appeared to be a couple of years older, and I realized I was seeing a moment from the future. Alyssa was in tears, shaking, and I was holding her and listening: "I don't want you and Mum to argue anymore, and be angry with each other. And I don't want Chiara to treat me like I don't exist. I want us to be together, happy, wherever we live. Together… Together…" I tried to comfort her. I looked at the wheels of our bikes, and how they kept spinning and spinning. I could not stop them. Just as I felt a choked scream stick in my throat, the scene vanished, and—*

I was at the table again, sitting across from D, who was bathed in the same gentle green light I had seen earlier in the meadow. The energy now washed over the table between us, even more intense than before. For several moments, I heard only the rhythm of my breathing and my heart beating. "She was worried about us. My little girl takes so much on her heart. What am I seeing here? Is my family going to fall apart?!" I searched for compassion and understanding in my friend's eyes.

Your heart was dreaming, and you saw its sorrows.

He reached forward and gently pushed the pad and paper to me.

Start here, now, with this.

Without questioning him further, I began writing down lines, ideas, impressions, as though I were capturing the shorthand of the heart:

*The Cabin*

*There are pointers everywhere, if your eyes are willing to see.*
*The people who have entered your life...*
*The experiences that have made you...*
*The dreams that inspire you...*
*The talents you have...*

*Do what opens and fills your heart with love.*
*Passion is the soul's way of letting the heart know what it wants.*
*Strip away emotional debris, and walk in great wonder and gratitude.*
*A full bank account and an empty heart are a poor bargain.*
*The comfort and material you seek will steal your life.*
*Dad was right: you won't take anything with you.*

*Time is a treasure; do not squander it.*
*The search for happiness is a fool's errand.*
*Joy is in your hands now, at this very moment.*
*This moment is all possible moments.*
*Give of your heart.*
*Give love.*

I sat back, put the pen down with a *whack*, and stared at D, my eyes wild and searching. "I want to be at peace with my past decisions and mistakes, and do the best for my family. Please, help me get there." I glanced at the windows and noticed the weather had changed: snow was falling. D leaned forward and put his large hands on the table.

Don't regret the past, the mistakes you think you've made, or the ventures you consider failures. And don't worry about the future. We're going to travel time together, and the more we do so, the more you'll realize the truth of what you just wrote.

Each experience can either harden or soften the heart. That's the choice you have. We need each other to heal and we all need a place to hide when we're hit by a storm. We all need love. That's why I am never homeless, because I live in my heart. The place you want to be.

48

*The Indomitable Silence*

He got up and started moving past the table, placing a hand on my shoulder as he opened the door with the other. Then he was out front and, just like that, he was gone into the snow squall, Glider following after him. Cold wind rushed into the cabin, but it didn't bother me. I then remembered what D had said earlier that morning, that by learning to dance in the rain we will find the peace to get through life's challenges and face the future with hope in our mind and faith in our heart. I tore off the top piece of paper, folded it, and placed it in my jacket pocket.

I stood up and stepped through the door. Just as I pulled it closed behind me, the storm front cleared as though at the snap of a finger, and the sun shone down on the mountainside. A wonderful singing silence washed down the slope. It was heavenly. Closing my eyes to let the rays warm and relax my tense face, I took a deep breath. As I exhaled, I opened my eyes and — boom! — I was sitting in my car in the parking lot of the park across the lake, the bustle and noise of the city almost deafening me!

It took what seemed an eternity to get my bearings and understand where I was. But I had learned to flow with strange events in recent months. The rumble of the engine seemed almost obscene to me after the mystery on the mountain, after the silence that had brought a hint of the truth to my heart. Soon, though, I reoriented myself to the reality of the car space, and pulled out of the park.

The mountain highway came up to meet me, like a looping movie clip. With destination unknown, I kept my foot steadily pressed against the accelerator. It felt thrilling, as though all things were possible. I drove and drove, tingling with excitement, until I lost track of time.

# A LAMP BURNS

How long I had been staring at the big screen, I didn't know. But there I sat, in my home theater, while a movie was playing. Something about guys riding their bikes through mountains in Europe. Their formation reminded me of starlings in their murmurations, moving with one mind. I looked down at my laptop. It appeared I had come here to work but had fallen asleep. Though confused, I could remember everything else from before. I had written many pages, finishing with a few lines expanding on the words from the cabin:

*I am the silence.*
*No matter the wars in your head.*
*No matter the clouds in your heart.*
*No matter the storms in your life.*
*I am beyond all that.*

I stopped, stared questioningly at these last words, and sat entranced for a while. Glancing at the computer, I saw the time was 5:10 a.m. again. Puzzled by this coincidence, I saved the document, set the laptop aside, and got up to brush my teeth. Fanny and the girls were still sleeping. *No yoga?* I thought to myself. *Strange.*

Putting on my boots and winter gear, I stepped out into the crisp morning air, which, as the day before, felt like a gentle slap in the face. Though it didn't feel as though any time had passed since then, I concluded it had been another clear night. The same amount of snow

*A Lamp Burns*

was still on the ground, and the sky was a soft purple-blue, though the sun had not yet risen over the mountains to the east. No traffic. Silence reigned all around me, disturbed only by my breathing and the gentle crunch of small stones and remaining snow underfoot.

Not knowing how far D's cabin was from my house, or if my current path connected with his, I just kept walking, confident that somehow I would find him, or he would find me. The valley unfolded before me, and I felt humble and grateful for its beauty and serenity. I would miss all this if we returned to the Netherlands, and I knew Fanny would. My girls were young and had their own plans and dreams. Chiara was planning to enter university, and Alyssa, like me, loved the culture of Europe. And yet I felt this increasing call back there. Unable now to sort out the future, my thoughts flashed back to my childhood days.

My dad often took me for walks in a nearby forest, which gave him the chance to teach me some life lessons along the way. One day he gave me a handwritten note in which he drew a picture of my life against the background of the four seasons. Through all my many moves, I had carried it with me in a box, oftentimes pulling it out and reading it over and over. After so many years, the words felt written right on the walls of my heart:

> *Spring is the period of birth, when nature starts to blossom. Animals leave their shelters to find fresh food in the woods, branches show their new green dresses, sweet little lambs play like fools in the meadows, and farmers sow their seeds for our daily bread. New life starts all around, and your heart is filled with new energy and freshness.*
>
> *In summer nature is in full bloom, at the top of its strength. Fields offer their gifts, gardens display their fragrant beauty, and people venture from their homes*

*The Indomitable Silence*

*to taste new cultures and experiences. And you and I are at our physical and emotional peak.*

*In autumn nature changes its colors and starts to lose its strength. Trees shed their leaves, windstorms rage, and rains leave their traces, forcing people indoors, as animals prepare their provisions for wintertime. This season is symbolic of the ups and downs in your life. It's the ideal period for you to turn inward and reflect in quiet contemplation.*

*In winter nature sleeps, almost looking dead, but in actuality it's living underground and readying for rebirth. Mother Earth dons her virgin white dress, as she sits with regal serenity, looking untouched by the pain and struggle of life. This soul is who you are in essence, my son. No matter how hard the storms hit, or how fragile your heart feels, you will always be this beautiful soul.*

*Your Dad.*

Reflecting on how my life was entering this autumnal time of contemplation, and feeling the air get a little cooler, I let my mind wander to other images of my youth. Winter afternoons spent sledding down a forest hill not far from where my father used to take me. I could clearly see the pathway across the foot of the run, beside a creek. We used to laugh with nervous excitement as we picked up the speed, and we knew we had to dig our feet into the ground to keep from launching ourselves into the ice-cold water.

My memories faded as a sudden warmth bathed the right side of my face. I looked eastward and saw the sun was rising, its beautiful orange glow cresting the mountains, preparing to command the valley. Sensing twenty minutes or more had passed, I stopped and looked around. Magically, I was on the same trail we had walked before. Mystifying to me was how I had never hiked this route before, nor seen his cabin, even after a few years of exploring this mountainside.

I could almost see it now, beyond the big clearing. With joyous anticipation, I continued walking, until his cabin peaked out from behind the rocky outcrop in the near distance. Stepping again over the pesky rock pile and the fallen trees, I broke into an easy stride and crossed the meadow. To my own surprise, I began whistling absently. As I focused my vision, I found him sitting on a wide tree trunk, an axe in his large hand. He was chopping wood. Smiling, I called out. My voice failed me at first, delivering a faint rasp. I cleared my throat and shouted louder, deciding to test his Dutch: "*Goede morgen, vriend*!" He turned and smiled.

A very good morning to you, sir!

Glider poked his scruffy head up from behind the wood pile and barked happily. "Hello, my little friend!" He came over and I scratched his ears, watching his little tail wag. "I feel wonderful, thank you. Preparing firewood, I see?" Glider went back and sat next to D.

Well, an old man needs some exercise to get his body going every morning. While I still can!

"So, this is the secret to staying in such great shape?"

Ha ha! I'll take that as a compliment. Yes, I think we need to train ourselves to keep in shape, not only physically but also mentally and emotionally. I have not forgotten the times I felt really miserable. They inspire me to keep pushing myself and not fall into the trap of complacency and laziness. Good health is a treasure. I'll never take that for granted again.

"Good point! I think we make the same mistakes in relationships and friendships. As long as we're together and everything is fine, we

*The Indomitable Silence*

almost take love for granted. But the moment the other person is no longer there, we realize how important they are to us and we miss them. We feel it! I experienced such a moment when my wife and our two girls went on holiday to Indonesia for two weeks. Although I drowned myself in work, I missed them every day, and when I finally saw my little ones running toward me at the airport in Amsterdam, I couldn't help but take them in my arms and cry with joy." I felt surprised at my sudden candor. Clearly my family was on my mind again.

Those moments are a great reminder that the most important lists to take care of are not our "to-do" lists but our "to-love" ones.

"So true but so easy to forget," I replied, thinking about the many times my busy schedule had taken me away from what matters most: loved ones, children, friends. He put down the axe and took out a pocket knife. He then picked one of the smaller pieces of kindling and began whittling. Neither of us spoke for a bit, as a gentle breeze mingled with the raspy sound of the blade on the wood. "What are you making?"

I don't know yet. The beauty of getting older is that it's not about the end result so much as the flow of intention. Like when you were a kid.

Recalling the many self-help books I had read in my twenties, I blurred it out: "Happiness for no reason!"

Because there is no reason! As long as you need a reason to be happy, you'll always find one not to be happy.

He stopped and winked at me. "Yes, but at my age some success does help. It pays the bills, you know." I found a nearby rock and sat down, looking at him with my elbows on my knees.

*A Lamp Burns*

Sure, resources give you options. But happiness is not something you squeeze from life; it's the very essence of who you are that opens itself up, flows outward, and enlightens everything it touches. Just like sunrays.

"I've heard that one before. But still, it's not easy to enjoy the sunshine when your stomach is empty."

When the stomach is empty, only one problem, food. But when the stomach is full, oh ... now many problems. Ha! You know how many people I've known who could buy anything they wanted, whose pockets were so full they could feed a whole village for the remainder of their days? Outwardly successful people, living in palatial homes and driving fancy cars, but inside restless, unhappy, searching for an elusive ... something?

For a moment he stopped whittling and raised his head, gazing at one of the nearby oaks whose branches nearly touched his little palace.

They think success bears the fruit of happiness and therefore do anything to become successful. But once they sit on their pile of achievements and stuff for too long, they'll find out success is more like a branch of the tree of happiness. You can work yourself into success, but you can't buy happiness. You can only access it when you turn inward and connect with your heart. What they're looking for is right under their nose!

"It's tragic, isn't it?"

It's tragic and funny at the same time. Happiness is so close, yet so far away. That's why they want to drive all these fast cars. So they will arrive on time! If only they knew where to go...

"Maybe you can show the way?"

Oh, who wants to listen to an old man who has nothing to show for?

*The Indomitable Silence*

"But you have something they don't. You are happy!"

You know when they're ready? When they reach a dead end, and there's nowhere else to go but turn around and take a different road. That's the value of a personal crisis.

"No pain, no gain," I said absently, my head already somewhere else. D's glassy eyes shot me a penetrating look. I felt exposed, naked, as if there was no place to hide my little secret.

I can see there's something on your mind.

I took a deep breath and felt a slight hesitation to talk about it, as I was still trying to wrap my mind around what exactly had happened. I started anyway. "It's strange, but when I was writing earlier, it felt like you were there! I remembered everything almost perfectly. I don't understand." Setting the wood and knife down beside him, he grinned at me.

We are connected, like fingers of the same hand.

I recalled the other realm I had traveled with Atmos, and the invisible cords connecting our spiritual bodies. But that was only between family members. D then took me by surprise again, revealing he had read my thoughts.

The cords you saw are stronger for relatives, but they can exist otherwise, when emotional bonds are strong. The universe is mystery upon mystery. Far beyond your cherished logic and the five senses.

"Just a few steps and a change in perspective unfolds, as you said the last time we were here. Wait, was that yesterday?" D folded the knife, put it together with the wood into his coat pockets, and appeared to ignore my question. I let it go.

*A Lamp Burns*

The world is seen through the mind's veil. You're continuously projecting your own thoughts, beliefs, images, and feelings, onto everything that meets the eye. That's how your own darn soap-reality movie is created! Perception is based on perspective, which is based on awareness. So ... speaking of steps, let's go inside and do some film editing, so to speak.

"That sounds lovely. Do you still have those cupcakes?" I smiled abashedly as he raised an eyebrow at me.

Ha! And I thought you were here to learn. It's really just the sweets you're after!

"Can't it be both?" He let out such a booming laugh that Glider barked. I was glad to see him so happy, and I was starting to see more clearly the simple grace of touching hearts. We went into the cabin and I took the same seat as before; his furry friend stayed out front. D went about preparing our coffees and getting some snacks. I closed my eyes and let my mind wander. Soon images appeared on an imaginary screen suspended above the table. Sensing what I was doing, he gave me instructions from across the room. Focusing on the lamp's flicker, I imagined its warmth opening a place in me for the words my friend was about to say.

Now turn on the light a little more. Make the images brighter, more intense, and feel how you're bursting with joy. Just take in the scenes and breathe in all the sensations.

As he spoke these words, a bright white light filled the space, but not from the window, from within, and it slowly became bigger and bigger until it lit up the whole screen in front of me. It was as if this light shone right through me and a wave of vibrant energy rolled through my body, which by now had become almost ethereal. I was seeing not with my eyes but with my heart.

*The Indomitable Silence*

Images came and went. I saw my father and mother as a young couple, hand in hand, surrounded by an ever-expanding light. An aura of soft colors was visible around their bodies, which were not solid forms but a transparent, vibrating mix of energies combined in a moving picture. Without speaking they smiled at each other, and their eyes radiated deep love. Though their lips weren't moving, I heard warm and soft sounds, and I thought to myself that if this was heaven, I wanted to be in this realm forever.

Then a small child entered the scene, and I could see myself as a little boy, eyes blue and shining, full of the peace and contentment I had lost in later years. Other childhood memories passed by like clouds floating in a clear blue sky: my first love when I was only five years old; walking alone down country lanes and fields of grass and grains; being bullied as a schoolboy; falling into a large swimming pool without knowing how to swim, my concerned brother watching nearby. Focusing on his face, I could feel his fear as if it were my own. Oddly enough, I could also sense the self-loathing in the hearts of those bullies as strongly as my own suppressed anger. It also became clear to me why it had all happened.

Those schoolkids were my guides from heaven, sent to strengthen my ability to deal with challenges and resistance. Breaking through the barrier of time, I saw the events were based on spiritual agreements made in the other realm, confirming what I had already learned from Michael and Atmos earlier that summer. Then images of my tennis period appeared. The joy of victory and the sadness of loss, like my other experiences, had not only happened *to* me, but even more so *for* me, to forge my willpower and self-discipline in the face of adversity — life skills that hadn't come naturally to me.

Re-experiencing these events, my emotions were more intense, more vivid, as though amplified right here in D's cabin. Then, to my shock, my eyes turned black and hollow, and I was right there, in the mud pool of my depression. To my relief, light-beings were carrying me,

*A Lamp Burns*

passing their love into my body's energy-field. I witnessed my own healing, the rebirth of my soul, preparing me for challenges and opportunities that were still ahead of me.

Faces of people I loved as well as faces of people who had played a harsher role in my past drifted by, and I could see their connection with my path. It was clear to me even the ones who had hurt me had come into my life for my benefit and growth. Nobody had come by accident and nothing had happened in vain. There was purpose, there was love, there was…

This light is who you are in your essence, brother.

His words seemed to split my consciousness, allowing me to see both past and present simultaneously. I could sense he was preparing our coffees in the kitchen, while I was still immersed in my own movie. I didn't answer, not wanting to lose the beautiful connection I was experiencing.

You're looking through the soul's eyes now, witnessing the heart's dreams, as happened in the scene with your daughter yesterday. You've always wondered what happens when you send love into the universe? Well, this is what it does. Love talks... Love talks...

"It all feels so real," I whispered softly, my eyes still closed.

It is real! Just a different reality than you're used to.

D's voice had become quite a bit louder now, and his last words pulled me fully out of the movie. I slowly opened my eyes, still electrified by my relived experiences, feeling like a resonating guitar string long after it's been plucked. I looked across the room; D had finished up in the kitchen.

You felt who you really are, because all that isn't the real you — the many thoughts and images, the emotions that are piled up, all that

*The Indomitable Silence*

you identify yourself with — was stripped away. And all there was left was the light. Nice, hey?

He walked back to the table, with a tray of coffees, glasses of water, and, this time, fruit and chocolate danishes. "That was beyond beautiful. Can I go back to that space?"

The light isn't yours, it only shines through you. It's the Source, the Heart of everything. And it's always there. Even if you are far away.

"But I felt it … I was part of that Heart!" D sat down, looked at me, and smiled.

Kind of reassuring, isn't it? Here, take some water — drink what you are.

"Ah … yes, we are for the most part water, as they say. Thank you." I gulped down the cool water like a man who had walked across a thousand miles of desert. With some left in the bottom, I held up the glass and took a casual look. But I did a double take when I noticed the water and the glass itself looked different, as if it were alive with tiny waves of energy moving endlessly, constantly pulsating, tossing, and rolling. "What…?"

Everything is alive. Even inert matter, like this glass and the table, contains moving energy. You are this energy, this intelligence, this consciousness, and for some moments it expanded far beyond your mind and body. Cool, isn't it?

"It actually felt like I had no boundaries. This light was … everywhere! And it seemed that I was … nowhere!"

Like the wave that collapses back into the surf and returns to the sea, when you experience your true nature, you lose the sense of a personal, separate self. Your soul and the Source of life are

*A Lamp Burns*

one: duality is only a matter of perspective. Now let that truth sink into your heart.

He paused and gave me a moment to align my heart with the words spoken, and the energy they were arising from. Then he continued.

The root of all the struggle and conflict between people is the false idea that we are separated from one another. We are all expressions of the One life, the One ocean, created by it, supported by it, and powerful because of it. If we would all realize this, we could never hurt one another.

He got up and opened all the windows, like last time, and again it created a familiar feeling of connection to something bigger than myself. We sat in silence for what seemed a long while, eating the danishes and fruit, and sipping our coffees, until it hit me. The words I had written before coming here! I lowered my mug mid-sip and stared at D. *I am the silence.... I am beyond all that.* "I ... I wrote that earlier." D grinned, blinked slowly, and bit his lower lip in delight at my realization.

Nice! Of course you did. I write some lines, you write some — everyone does. We're all actors in the One Big Movie that never ends. And like in a sci-fi movie, almost anything can be done with a heart burning with passion, and some common sense. So expect the unexpected. You've heard the expression "going beyond the fourth wall"?

"Yes, when the camera goes behind its perspective and *that* becomes part of the story."

Exactly. So, then, look behind you!

I placed my mug on the table and turned my chair around. The wall with the door was gone! Well, it wasn't so much gone as I could see through it as though it were suspended plasma, allowing me to see the

*The Indomitable Silence*

meadow beyond. And to my utter astonishment, I didn't see just one dog but two: Glider and Cinnamon, both playing together, creating a vibrating ball of white, brown, and grey fur. It was a display of unleashed canine joy. They barked, jumped, scampered, rolled, and looked about as content as any two dogs ever could. I turned back to look at D, wide-eyed with delight.

We are not the only ones connected, clearly! Ha ha. I wanted our dogs to play, so I called it up in my heart and shared it with you. I knew they would get along. This is where my dreams come true ... or just entertain me for a while. And you thought the cabin was just about coffee and dessert!

"I want to do more of this kind of magic! And I want to be just like them. They look so happy!"

Without jumping and rolling on people, I would hope! Ha ha.

"Well of course! I meant pure joy, pure connection, playfulness. Expressing my true nature."

Then free yourself from all these false identifications: a tennis player, a business man, an introvert, or whatever else you think you are. They were part of your paintings, but they are not the painter. You were quite comfortable in these roles for a while, and they even gave you a certain sense of pleasure and success, but the time has come to move beyond them.

He was throwing some curveballs at me. I sensed there were more to come.

All this was an expression of you, but they are not your essence. Figurative waves that, like real ones, will crash and return to the ocean — who you really are. That's why we love dogs! They are not lost in their minds. They just ARE themselves, without trying to be.

I turned again and looked for the dogs, but all I saw was the door and the wall. "And then what?"

People are already painfully aware of their limitations; they want to hear what's possible beyond that! Remind them of what they have forgotten; that they, too, are an inseparable part of the ocean. And not only tell them, but show them by being the example of what you teach. That's your unique talent and it's what your heart craves for more than anything else. That's what you're supposed to do. Then the emptiness inside will leave, and the fullness of your being will shine in all its beauty. Just like the sun.

We finished our danishes and coffees, and I looked out the window to see the sun now fully visible over the distant mountains. I had lost track of time, but I resisted the urge to look at my iPhone. For a moment I felt the serenity I used to experience when I was a young man, when I would sit on a park bench after work and watch people walk by, immersed in the feeling that I didn't want to be anywhere else. Only now I had a companion.

Let's walk.

We ventured out. What a beautiful day! Already the warmth of the sunlight was baking the mountainside, and I could hear the rush of water falling into a canyon behind a high ridge. "I've never walked over there, though I've always wanted to."

The Rim, they call it. It's a beautiful place.

As we made our way farther up the trail, I saw D's face glowing and vibrant, and his grey hair looked like golden threads in the shining sun. Glider came bounding from behind and caught up with us, panting. His playing with Cinnamon had obviously tired him out. D patted his head absently, looking out at the snow-covered peaks and the still-green valleys between them, letting the breeze move over him.

*The Indomitable Silence*

Isn't this staggering? Nothing reminds me more of our connection to one another and to nature than this view does. So wonderful to be immersed in this beauty, with you.

I paused and tried to take in the beauty of Mother nature, but my analytical mind had already taken place in the space she presented. "We don't always treat nature that kindly. Actually we've made a mess, and we're already paying a huge price."

We treat Mother Earth as we treat ourselves, which is often with neglect and abuse. We forget she's a living being, like us. She smiles when happy, she shivers when troubled, and she throws up when sick. We need to take good care of her. She only lives once.

Images of natural disasters floated through my mind while we walked a little farther, until we reached a scrubby sub-alpine area covered in clusters of bright wildflowers. We sat down, my mind still grappling with what D had said about this sense of connectedness and oneness. "I know conceptually we are all one, but I still often catch myself feeling separate from everything around me. I am here, you are there, and the mountains are even farther away. I don't always feel as one. I'm trying, but…"

D rose and walked to a nearby bush, where he bent over and picked a flower. Recognizing its four petals of soft yellow and orange, I realized I had seen this species before at high altitudes in the Rockies. It was a Western Wallflower. Though I was surprised to see so many of them still thriving in November, I knew by now not to question such oddities. He returned and sat down beside me, the flower in his open palms as if he were in devotional prayer.

It's beautiful, isn't it? This piece of life.

I nodded in silence. He closed his eyes, brought the flower to his nose, and inhaled deeply. A delighted smile appeared on his face.

*A Lamp Burns*

Here, your turn.

He stretched out his hands and the flower glided into mine. As I closed my eyes, a powerful feeling of peace flowed deep within me, as it seemed the flower's essence had nestled in my heart and become one with mine. I sensed her beauty, her aliveness. D also must have sensed I wanted to cherish this moment as long as I could, as he didn't say a word. Finally, after what felt like a long time, his soft, gentle voice broke the silence.

What fragrance is to a flower, love is to a human being. The flower doesn't try to smell sweet or look beautiful. She just is! And so, love is not an act of will; it's not something you can practice and become good at. It's a state of being, what remains if you lay down all your clothes. And I don't mean that literally!

"Ha ha! No worries. I'm not gonna embarrass myself in front of an old man. I do have my pride, you know." I just loved his dry and quirky sense of humor. And even while he was sharing so many gems of wisdom, he could unexpectedly throw in these pebbles of laughter.

By now my eyes were open again, and my fingers settled gently on the flower's petals as a bee might. I could still feel their energy mingling, like an excited whisper between friends, and I smiled at D. "Something is glowing inside me."

In your heart there's a silent voice no one else but you can hear. Jesus said so beautifully: "The Father and I are one. He who has seen me, has seen the Father." The One has expressed Himself in the many, and the many know they are all one. This is the ultimate realization. You are still in the waves, but the ocean's depth is only one dive away. Love is one heartbeat away. That's why I keep my cabin windows open, to remind me. It's not just for fresh air!

*The Indomitable Silence*

We both stood up and continued along our path. By his brisk pace I could tell he was getting very excited, and I had a hard time keeping up. I looked at the back of D's head, and for a split second I could have sworn he was my father, with me on one of our nature walks. My throat filled with longing and my eyes with tears as I tapped him on the back. He turned around and, a little disappointed, I saw D's face. "For a moment I thought you were my…"

Father?

"Yes."

Well, not only Jesus had a Father. Uh … in the flesh, I mean. Ha ha!

He picked up the pace even more, to the point where I was getting almost exhausted. "Can't we stop for a moment? And I could really use some cold, fresh water."

Oh, come on! These long legs should do what they're supposed to do. Walk, and if needed, run! Watch out!

A small snake made its sneaky appearance from behind a bush, slowly slithering in our direction. It freaked me out, and in the snap of a finger I was at a safe distance. Looking at D, I found him smiling, still keeping the same pace, apparently unconcerned by our little visitor's presence.

See, where is your tiredness now? Obviously a snake can do miracles. Ha! Speaking of water, can you hear the waterfall getting louder? We're close.

I shook my body, just like Cinnamon does when he comes out of the water, as if to shake off the remaining fright, and focused my ears on what was ahead. I wondered why I hadn't noticed the sound before.

*A Lamp Burns*

Perhaps my fear of the snake had numbed my senses. "Wow, what a sound, so powerful!" D winked at me as though to say, it always is.

Before I realized, the three of us were on the edge of a raised precipice, looking down into a shockingly deep canyon. The water roared into rocky channels beyond sight. We leaned over, D with his hand protectively on Glider. Our hair, and fur, was tousled by a sudden gust of wind that came ripping over the mountain peak to our west.

This beautiful canyon was once carved by the natural forces of life, of water, and the intention of the universe. Life is always looking for expansion, the soul for evolution. Many people ask themselves why life puts them in the path of the rushing water, but it's much more helpful to wonder at its beauty and embrace the opportunity to be part of it. We're all co-creators, and seen through the soul's eyes we are whole. Nothing is missing or broken, even though it might appear so on the surface.

D was silent for a long while, his hands clasped in front of him. We took in the thunderous sound and watched the spray flying high above the falls. These effects seemed to buoy D for what he was about to say.

A long time ago I had a dream which made such an impact on me that I still remember it as if it were last night. I saw a little boy with no arms and legs, sitting on the ground and writing with a pen in his mouth. I didn't want to disturb him, so I watched in silent admiration as he moved effortlessly across the paper. When he finally noticed me, he angled his head, dropped his pen with great care, and stared at me. He was all smiles! A peace entered my heart I can't describe, and tears came rolling down my cheeks. It wasn't that I felt sorry for him. No, the tears came from a fountain of joy he had somehow touched in me.

*The Indomitable Silence*

This same fountain speak to me now as words of bliss bubbled up in my mind:

*I count my blessings, not my tears; my opportunities, not my challenges.*
*I am grateful for all life has given me, but also withheld from me.*
*I always have the opportunity to smile and be happy.*
*And I have chosen to do exactly that.*

*I have hope and faith, because I feel a sense of purpose in my heart.*
*I know deep within I am perfect in spite of all my imperfections.*
*All is well, I am well, for I am beloved by My Father.*
*And I hope one day I can see myself as He sees me.*

This little guy had found the source of happiness within. He became the light, and then enlightened others. He took every moment as an opportunity to express himself as the person he wanted to be, and to find ways he could touch people's hearts. Look at how he touched my heart, even in a dream! Such a smile. Such strength in his joy.

I watched the column of water roar into the rocks below, sending a contrasting light mist halfway up to us. Several moments passed as I took in the sight and sound of the falls, drawing a parallel between the water and the boy. Both flowed with a power that seemed unstoppable. "That's what I want!" My eyes were still on the canyon as D spoke.

You've learned some lessons the hard way, but now it's time to let go and look forward, feeling possibilities in each moment. With hope and faith in your heart. Yes, for heaven's sake, let go of that judgment — of yourself or anyone else.

"Not always easy to quiet the chatter in my head, though."

I know all too well, brother. We've spent too much time in this mental garbage bin, you and I; telling ourselves the same old stories over and over. See that water. That rushing, frothing torrent is like

*A Lamp Burns*

society with all its people. Sometimes you are in the ocean depths, and other times you must reach out into the raging tumult of life. Believe me, everyone in that waterfall has felt alone. But you are not alone; we all go back to the ocean. Together.

"We just take different paths through the rocks."

And there's no right or wrong way. So move ahead and let go of the burden you've carried with you for too long. Shake it off! Like little Glider here!

Glider looked at him, woofed, and then squinted contentedly as D scratched his ears.

As the years passed, you've taken on more and more coats which covered the pureness of your spirit. Jesus reminded us to be like children before we enter the kingdom of heaven. The return to innocence.

"Thank you for all that you share with me. I'm so grateful."

No thanks necessary. I'm at peace with where I am and who I am. It's a wonderful place to be. And I want the same for you.

As I turned back to face the waterfall, I noticed a tear fall from my face, down and down, into the canyon, into D's metaphorical society, with all its sadness and hope, its fear and love.

And all its flaws and grace. All its oneness.

He had read me again. I returned my gaze to him. "All its oneness."

What I am, you are. We are, One.

He pushed himself up from the edge of the cliff with an alarming burst of energy, and started dancing around the nearby flat area like

*The Indomitable Silence*

a little kid, his arms in the air, feet off the ground, a crazed smile on his face. Glider barked happily, while I just sat there and admired his lust for life. He reached his hand out to me, inviting me to jump with him, and so I did. Soon I was overcome by unbridled joy; I hadn't laughed that way for a long time. He then hugged me, and rather than feeling awkward, I felt more alive than I had in years.

Life is awesome!

"You're one of a kind, D."

And so are you! Unique and beautiful as you are.

His words jumped right into my heart, and a wave of self-acceptance washed through me, as though cleansing grime from cracks and crevices. "You paint a picture of a man in his twenties!"

I feel younger right now than I did fifty years ago.

I thought of my own early twenties and how my mind was dark and clogged with pain and fear, trapped by old hurts and hijacked by worries.

Surrender... Let go... Have a little faith.

Thinking this might be one of his literal-versus-figurative jokes, I let go of him physically. "What about my resentments?" Unfazed, D picked up Glider and began dancing with him, laughing. The little pooch licked his face and looked around, a little confused.

Embrace your resentments! Bring them into your heart where they can melt into the ocean of love. Just as ice turns into water when touched by the sun. Surrender to love as I have! You know that's the answer.

I knew he was right, and I made a promise to myself. Never again would I waste another moment of precious life. I wanted to be free.

Free from fear. And live! Just then the water behind him began rushing with greater force, pushing a massive cloud of spray higher and higher, until it was behind D and Glider like a backdrop of a theatrical stage. Soon it began falling on them, obscuring them more and more while D continued speaking.

Dance in the mist, my friend! That water is all of us, doing the work and creating the canyons on the mountain. And these tiny droplets are like those who have found their highest vibration of love. They have surrendered, and look at how high they fly as they do their happy work. Join us!

And then they were gone! I leapt to the edge of the cliff, fell on my knees, and gripped its rocky edge. There was no sign of them. I strained to see into the canyon below, but I couldn't make out any details. "They can't have jumped!" I whispered fiercely to myself. "This can't be..." I put my head down on my arms and closed my eyes. Then I noticed something very strange. My heavy breathing and rapid heartbeat seemed to match the rhythm of the rushing water perfectly. I felt myself joining the water; that I *was* the water! There was no distance between. I could feel the energy coursing through me, washing away my thoughts, taking me away.

Of course I didn't jump! Ha ha. I didn't mean surrender life, but surrender TO it.

I jolted upright and looked straight ahead. But instead of rock and dirt, I saw the wooden table, the coffee mugs and plates, the pad and pen to my left. D was across from me, grinning, petting Glider on his lap. Rather than address the bizarreness of it all, I drilled down on one detail. "Glider is inside. Don't you normally leave him out in front of the cabin?"

My leaps through time and space scare him sometimes. He was whimpering a bit, so I brought him in. Well, how do you feel?!

*The Indomitable Silence*

"Like somewhere between you and Glider, in terms of my cosmic comprehension!" D let out a roaring laugh to rival the roar of the waterfall. He then set his furry, loyal buddy on the floor, leaned forward, and gave me a riveting stare.

*But you feel something more, don't you? Something much deeper. I've felt that, too. I was a father...*

I took a deep breath and placed my hands on my knees. "It feels like when I held Chiara and Alyssa in my arms for the first time. I was in the hospital and there was this ocean of emotions washing through me, which I couldn't control. It was beautiful beyond words. Never had I felt anything like that before."

*Intense, and different from the love a man has for his wife.*

He looked at me, not invasively but knowingly, and I could sense he knew our family had been having difficulties lately. We stared silently at each other, before I spoke again. "I think family life is the most challenging love of all. It takes a lot of patience and perseverance, and wisdom, and there can be conflict between our mutual needs and desires. How do you balance those? Sometimes I just don't know what love wants me to do."

*That is something you can only answer, but in your heart, not in your head. And not in one conversation. This one may take you some time.*

Finding a window of relief in D's last comment, I took a breath and grinned at him. "Is that why you left a note in my mailbox, to get me asking these questions and seeking answers?"

*Well, yes... And I wanted someone to join me for a hike, and have some coffee and dessert with me.*

He winked and smiled so warmly that I knew his friendship and support would always be with me. He gently picked up Glider, calmly walked out the door and disappeared. A breeze entered the cabin and whirled softly around me, fluttering the pages on the pad. I reached for the pen, rolled it again between my thumb and finger, and began writing:

*A day comes in your life when, in the throes of all your pain and suffering, you reach the end of your rope, and a screaming voice cries out loud. You want no more of this! You're done battling the world outside and shutting down the demons inside. You've done everything you could, but it feels like it got you nowhere.*

*Nothing seems to go your way, not even prayer, and you feel forsaken, hurt, lost. Then, like the blue sky after an outburst of thunder and lightning, you blink back your stinging tears, lean back and relax, take a few deep breaths, and begin to see the world through fresh, clear eyes.*

I gently set the pen down on the table, stood up, looked around the room, and then went out the door. Slowly making my way back home, I easily found the trail that had brought me here. With every footstep I saw memories about our recent meeting and the ones prior. It was a lot to take in, and I feared I might forget most of it. I knew many more questions were still lingering in my mind, and I didn't know if I would ever have the chance to ask him all of them. But somehow it didn't seem to matter. It wasn't about having all the answers but about feeling my heart in the moment. Something deep within was shifting. A *new me* was gradually being born.

Tired but fulfilled, I arrived at my house and opened the front door. Inside, Fanny and the girls were sitting in the living room, watching Netflix. They all looked up at me as Cinnamon came running, and my heart filled to the point of bursting with love.

# TEARS IN HEAVEN

"Do you believe in Jesus?"

His axe came down with such precision and confidence that I thought he may be more than just a liaison, as he described himself. He didn't answer right away, but with measured movements took up the fresh firewood from either side of the chopping block and placed it atop the growing cord next to the cabin. I helped him, grabbing an armful myself. I didn't press him nor back off from the topic. I had learned over the years to trust those moments when thoughts seem to come out of the blue, as they often lead to the most meaningful conversations.

I believe in love.

"That's not really an answer." The rigor of the moment called for a more challenging tone on my part. Also, I was feeling even freer around him since the waterfall incident, as his strength and boldness were beginning to rub off on me.

Oh yes, it is! Jesus was a living example of someone who showed us that we can only love God by loving people, even those who've left a trail of scars behind. I've tried to forgive, to be compassionate, but I've never succeeded in doing so by using the mind only. Not until I fell into my heart space did grace open me up to a love I never knew existed.

*Tears in Heaven*

"Do you believe Jesus is the only way to God, as Scripture tells us?"

If that were true, then what about all those people who are good at heart and do well to others, yet live in societies where Christianity isn't the main religion? Will they be judged by their beliefs, or rewarded because of the fruits of their lives? What do you think?

"I think it's not about strictly following the laws and rules laid out for us, but about living from the heart and inspiring others to do the same." He picked up the axe and was about to grab another full piece to split, when he stopped and looked me in the eye.

His life showed us what love looks like and his words expressed how love sounds. Unfortunately, people have distorted some of his messages, through poor translations, misinterpretations, and political agendas, and made something different out of them. Something that serves their thirst for power and control rather than feeding people's hunger for spiritual food.

"When I read certain passages in the New Testament, I feel their truth strongly resonating in me, and believe those words have actually been spoken by Jesus. But there are other passages where I don't feel that. And yet some would say we can't pick and choose from Scripture. We either believe it all or we don't, that there's no middle ground, no compromise, no choice."

With a small but forceful swing, he sank the edge of the axe into the block. In the warmth of some welcome sunlight, he rolled up his sleeves, and I could see his sinewy forearms were veiny from work and age. And his face was a bit contorted with annoyance. D was having an off-day. I sensed strong experiences were coming today.

I'm asking you, if there's no free choice, is there true freedom? And can there be love if there's no freedom?

"No, I don't think so."

*The Indomitable Silence*

Then why would the embodiment of love force you to believe anything, without questioning or further investigating?

"That's a very good question. I don't think he would."

All he talked about was God's love, and that the truth will set you free. So, how do you travel this road toward what he called "His Heavenly Father"? I believe the only way is the one that goes straight through the heart. That's where you can be with him, feel him, not in your head. And I don't believe he said that he, as a person, was the only way. I think he meant that love is the only way.

"I've seen things, with Michael, which I wrote about. I can't fully understand all of them, but I know they are true. So I see what you mean. Still…"

Still here you are, struggling and wondering how best to live given what you've seen and experienced. Do you remember what Michael said about the sun and the sunray? God's love is both, the source and its manifestation. And you are part of that. We are all rays of the one sun.

"And Jesus was the brightest of them all." D nodded and lined up another piece of wood to chop. He swung and split it as deftly as he had the other one, and watched as the pieces fell to either side of the chopping block. After losing himself in quiet contemplation for several seconds, he spoke calmly and thoughtfully, as though now soothed by the clarity of an inner knowing he'd forgotten.

When you enter the silence in the depth of your heart, you'll know where the kingcom is.

"*Be still and know that I am God.* A beautiful line from Scripture." D grinned, stood tall and straight, and looked at me with disarming tranquility in his eyes.

*Tears in Heaven*

Yes ... it certainly is. And its beauty lies in the fact we can all go there, to the kingdom, regardless of our particular beliefs. Just be still, open, and receptive to grace.

Before I had a chance to feel silly for asking him, the words came tumbling out of my mouth: "Have you...? Have you ever been there and had a personal experience with him? With Jesus?" His grin widened.

I was with him. In one of my dreams.

"In one of your dreams..." D smiled as he appeared to relive this profound and precious memory, while I pondered his response. Then, almost at the snap of finger, he became excited and animated like a little kid. He picked up the new pieces of kindling, tossed them haphazardly onto the cord, and turned to me, his hands high in the air.

Hey, why don't we?

"Why don't we what?"

Share the dream I've had! Of heaven! Like your cosmic friends who took you to the other side of the veil. This is nothing new for you.

"I know, but — we can actually meet him?"

We'll get to Jesus later. First I have to get you re-accustomed to the other realm. Let's go!

I could see how much this experience must have meant to him, as his face shone with anticipation and his voice cracked with tenderness. "You're not joking, right?" Hearing this, D became grouchy again.

Do I look like I'm messing with you?

*The Indomitable Silence*

"No, but——-"

No "but"! This is not a fancy fairy-tale! This is about truth, your truth, and it will help you find your way here on Earth. This is the way to ... the silence. Be prepared for a bumpy ride, though. Ready?

"Okay ... what do you want me to do?" He put the axe on the block and motioned for me to follow him into the cabin. Glider looked up as we passed him by the door. We entered and sat down at the wooden table, which still had used plates and mugs on it. D's face showed seriousness mingled with robust belief, like a sports coach. My thoughts were racing.

Strap in and be still. Close your eyes and focus on your breath.

I did as instructed, and after some time the traffic in my head gradually slowed down and got quieter. Although my mind was still somewhat unsettled, a burning desire to return to the other side was taking over my heart. And these feelings took me on a ride deep within.

You're doing great, brother. I can see it from here. It's working!

I was no longer seeing with my eyes but what my heart was dreaming. A presence, a sensation came over me, an inexplicable sense of calmness and serenity. And yet, I didn't see anything unusual; no bright light, no angels, no tunnel, no spirits of deceased loved ones. Just as he was about to tell me to keep focusing on my breath, it happened.

Bang! I was thrown backwards and out of my body, and before I could get my bearings, I realized I was peering through bright green light at two men sitting with their eyes closed. "Oh my goodness!" I wasn't saying these words out loud, but in silence, through my heart. "What just happened?"

*Tears in Heaven*

You left your body, and she helped you with it.

"She?"

Your angel! Sometimes there are two or three. You went through this in the summer, with Atmos, but you may have forgotten. Anyhow, you will remember this time.

"Fanny wouldn't like this—"

She need not worry. It's purely celestial, and all business. This is their work, to accompany people on a journey beyond time and space. What wife doesn't want her husband to grow in love and clarity? Now, hang on, here we go!

The awareness of being *me* was even deeper than in my daily consciousness. I felt set free, no longer trapped in my bodily sensations and mental prison. The veil that clouded my true essence was lifted and I felt loved. In fact, I was love! I was light! And this light was expanding more and more, as I could go anywhere I wanted. There were no boundaries, no limitations. I seemed to hover in this state for a while.

You needed some time to get used to your new body. You're ready now.

I rose through the roof as though it didn't exist, the angel's hand guiding me. Though I was now out of my physical body, everything still felt so real, so familiar. Looking down at my chest, I became aware of my heartbeat. My senses were intact, but the sounds were clearer, the smells more penetrating, and the colors brighter and more vibrant. I remembered this feeling! When I looked to the left, I saw D's astral body radiating brilliantly; it was about the same shape and size as the one he had left behind in his chair, but the edges were

*The Indomitable Silence*

less distinct, and it was hard to see where his body stopped and mine started. It was wondrous!

*The brightness of the light-body represents the intensity of love we have gathered in our being. And the higher we rise in love, the deeper we can access the truth. There's nowhere to hide, no mask to cover our true face.*

"Well, the light you emanate is obviously brighter than mine." I felt a little envious that he seemed to have integrated more love than me.

*Don't get silly here, it's not a contest! I'm also a little older, so you still have some time to catch up. Ha ha. Now stay with me. We will travel fast.*

And there I was in the hospital, walking through walls and moving with nothing but my imagination, until I arrived at a well-lit emergency room where the victim of a horrific accident had just been wheeled in. There was blood everywhere and I could see the person's body being hooked up to the EKG machine. Fortunately, there was no flatline, and I heard the doctor tell the two nurses to prepare for surgery. When I looked closer I saw it was a little boy. Outside the room his mother was waiting, completely overcome by grief and panic. I felt the desperation racing through her heart and heard her fervent prayers, as she begged God not to take her son but her instead, asking for forgiveness for all she had done wrong in her life.

I went back to the emergency room without opening the door to get in, and what I saw next was almost beyond what words could convey. Three angelic spirits glided down through a mist of purple and blue, accompanied by a man who appeared to be in his forties. While the mystical trio hovered above the young boy's body, the man stepped forward and laid his left hand upon the youngster's forehead. Healing beams came out of his hand and streamed into the child. I didn't

*Tears in Heaven*

recognize who he was, but something told me this was his dad and that he had died a couple of years earlier.

Just then, as the doctor was injecting the anesthetic, I heard the lad say, "Mummy! Mummy!" His dad took one of the nurses by the arm, and she immediately responded by opening the door and calling the mother in. "Mummy, I've seen him." His voice was already quite faint as the narcosis had started to kick in. "Who have you seen, honey?" the mother answered through her heart-rending sobs. "I..." His dad now bent over and kissed him gently on his forehead. "It's Dad, he's ... here!" His words had just enough power to reach his mother's ears, but I could see them falling apart in her mind. She thought he was hallucinating from the medication. And even though her husband wrapped his arms around her shoulders and laid his head against hers, she couldn't feel his presence.

Then I was pulled into a scene where the woman was driving an old blue Chevy, her six-year-old son sleeping in the backseat. Suddenly a black pick-up truck careened through a red light and plowed into the left side of her car. There was no way she could have escaped the collision. The driver, drug-addled and drunk at the time of the accident, died right away, and I could see how a few grey shadows arrived on the spot to take him away. There was a lot of screaming and cursing, and I tried to see where they were going, but they blurred into a nasty fog in the lonely distance.

While the mother tried to free herself, the little one lay nearly strangled by his seat belt. His dad then came from above, surrounded by a cloud of light and accompanied by three light-beings. They freed the boy, who by now had lost consciousness. For a moment, the father and son gazed upon each other with an intimacy and love my heart will never forget. Briefly, the curtain between this world and the hereafter was lifted, and their hearts merged into one.

*The Indomitable Silence*

After this scene, I was back in the hospital, where the boy was still lying on the operating table. The surgery was done, the doctor and two nurses were talking solemnly, and a few others were cleaning up. The attempt to save him had been unsuccessful. It wouldn't be long. The boy opened his eyes one more time and looked at his dad, who had been beside him all the while. The glow on the child's face matched that of the angels'. Then his father leaned forward and laid his cheek against his son's head. Tears of joy and sadness ran down his face as he whispered in his ear: "I love you, son. I'm with you. It's time for us to go now."

Soft but powerful music caressed my ears, as the voices of the three angels — one tenor, one bass, and one soprano — melted into a serene symphony. It was a song of praise celebrating the life God had given the boy. They wrapped his little body in a protective blanket of loving energy to ready him for his transition to the other side. His eyes were closed. Then an invisible hand guided me into direct communication with him, and I could hear his unspoken words: "I'm not afraid. I'm going home!" A wan smile appeared on his face. I looked at his mother to see if she had noticed the change in his physical appearance, but the tears made it impossible for her to see. "I'm so sad for Mum," the boy continued. "I know her heart is broken and life will never be the same for her again. I wish she could see I'm all right!"

"Can't you make her see you, or feel you?" I asked him. "Her heart isn't sensitive enough to feel, her ears aren't open enough to hear, and her eyes aren't clear enough to see," the boy replied. "She has her own journey to walk. I will help her as much as I can, but now it's my time to go. I'm ready." These words were no longer those of a child, but of an old soul; a soul that was at home with God.

The moment had arrived. Like steam from a tea pot, his astral body rose and left gently from the top of his head. The angels were still singing when his dad took him by the hand. He was finally free from

*Tears in Heaven*

the pain and wounds of his fragile body, and smiled with such radiant beauty! The purity of their love told me just how wonderful our world would be if we could all experience this heavenly love. Streams of wonder and bliss swirled through me as the boy, his father, and the three angels glided upward and disappeared, leaving mother alone with a waterfall of tears.

Isn't it beautiful to see there's no such thing as death?

"This is heartbreaking but so wonderful! I was there with them. In the hospital, in the car, even in their heads and hearts!" I looked down at my chest and was surprised to see it glowing with rich green light. I looked at D and saw his heart space was doing the same.

I know, I know. I was with you all the time. Fortunately, it's only softening your heart, not breaking it.

"I wish everyone could see this. I had caught glimpses of eternity before, but I never thought I would see it again."

That's why I'm reaching out, to remind you the soul is beyond time and space. This is the truth people need to hear. And though many have yet to open their hearts and minds to the boundless beauty beyond human imagination, many are starting to do so.

"I hope so."

It's happening, but slowly. Were it to happen too quickly, many people's minds would blow up and their hearts would stop beating from shock! Those who are sensitive enough are the first to see, for they're the ones who believe before they see. And when they share what they've seen, one day enough people will be reached for the truth to be revealed to all those who don't believe before they see.

*The Indomitable Silence*

"Michael and Atmos spoke of vibrational energy, of accumulating love, of preparing for life after our last breath."

Everything we experience on Earth either reinforces the light in us or diminishes it, and the intensity of this light determines where we are going and how it will be.

"The boy knew his end was near. And he was totally at peace with it. So beautiful to watch."

He was tuned into the higher vibrations of the spiritual realm; that's why he could see and hear his dad, and communicate with you while he was still in his body. Children are naturally very sensitive and open, but as they grow older they rise from the heart into the head, get caught in a cobweb of mental tricks and illusions, and lose their awareness of the eternal. The heart is still telling the truth, but who's listening?

"I feel sad about his mum and that she wasn't aware of what was going on. It would have comforted her knowing her son was free from pain."

It's always harder for the bereaved. You saw how worried the boy was about his mother and wanted nothing more than to shout that he was alive. And how different she would have felt if only she had known the man she had loved was with her and her boy. So many close their hearts to what's beyond the veil of physical death, identified with their physical vessel, clinging to earthly experiences and possessions. Some who have crossed the line don't even realize they are dead. They talk, but no one hears. They reach out, but no one feels. They shout, but no one seems to care. Prisoners of their own nightmares! If only they knew how close their loved ones are... Look, to the right!

*Tears in Heaven*

I looked down over my right shoulder. I had no recollection of having left the hospital, but there was no denying we were now hovering above the city park. I saw benches and the tents of the homeless in clusters, but strangely no one seemed to be around. The vegetation was sparse, as it was during my first meeting with D. I felt myself drawn to a particular tree, and I knew this was the spot I was supposed to focus on. Then I saw him. An old man's spirit sleeping against the back of a tree, covered in a grey haze of mist. When I looked closer, a tremendous fear grabbed me by the throat, almost strangling me. The man was sick and very weak. He reminded me a bit of D the last time I was here. My heart was heavy.

Hang on, brother. Focus on your inner light.

I felt myself slipping away, but his warning came just at the right time. I focused on my heart and after a few seconds regained my strength, sensing the green glow emanating from within me. "This is awful. Can't you wake him up?" D shook his head. "Why not?"

Because I can't reach him.

"But we can't just watch and do nothing! We need to help him!"

Be patient. Help is on its way. Look...

Beside the old man a young and healthy-looking fellow appeared, with an aura of violet and blue colors. I hadn't seen him coming, and it looked like he had materialized himself on the spot. Then, to my surprise, he started talking to the old man. "My brother in spirit, I have come to wake you up; it's time to go." His voice was soft but firm, and the old man opened his eyes bewilderedly. "Leave me alone," he said. "I want to stay here. I'm waiting for my wife. She must be here somewhere."

"No, you don't understand. You are dead! And your wife isn't coming. It's not her time yet." The young man's answer didn't calm him down, and the old man shouted, "I said leave me alone! Haven't you heard me?" His desperation and anger were palpable throughout my entire body. "I have come to guide you to a better place where you can rest for a while," said the young man evenly. "A place where you aren't haunted by nightmares or surrounded by shadows of lonely and desperate people."

"How do you know I have nightmares? Who are you? Why are you talking about shadows?" The old man shifted restlessly on the ground, glaring up at the younger man, who gently laid his left hand upon the old man's shoulder. I watched in relief and awe as a beam of green light passed into his heart, before the visitor continued in a compassionate tone. "Trust me. I know you well, but I can't help if you won't let me. Please, come with me. You are safe."

A gentle smile appeared on his earnest face, and I admired him for staying so calm and kind against so much hostility and fury. "I am not dead!" protested the old man. "Do you think I'm crazy, or what?" Soon his expression transformed from anger to vulnerability, as more rays of light entered the man's heart.

"I lived just like you," said the young man, "so I know what you're going through. In the throes of depression, I lost myself completely in the false companionship of alcohol and drugs. It was hard for me when I first realized I hadn't left my sorrows behind after stepping out. It was even more painful than all my experiences before." Shocked by this story, the old man raised himself, tenderness in his eyes, a lump in his throat. "You ... committed suicide?"

"Yes, at least that's what I thought I did. But when I regained consciousness it gradually dawned on me that my misery was not over. I had not truly crossed over. My mission to leave had failed!"

"Oh my God! What happened next?"

*Tears in Heaven*

"I found myself in a nasty place, where nothing breathed life. No trees, no greenery, no flowers. No roads, no bridges, not even homes. The barren landscape was filled with sharp, black rocks beside the long, muddy trails, and ditches with grey, foul water. It was freezing cold and this endless, thick, nasty fog made it almost impossible to look farther than ten feet ahead. And these awful smells — penetrating every cell of your body! Everyone wandered around nervously and blindly, as if haunted by invisible shadows, with no sense of direction or purpose. Pale, desperate, worn-out faces with lifeless expressions, and hollow eyes staring into the distance, devoid of any hope and joy. Nobody made eye contact. No sign of any shared affection whatsoever.

"I felt like I didn't exist, except for the ones who shouted at me, calling me names: 'suicide, weakling, loser.' The icy cold of deep loneliness sucked all the life out of me. There was no one to talk to, to laugh with, to listen to, except the screaming voices in my head. Torturing memories of heartaches; everything I wanted to escape from was even worse here. There was never a moment of peace or relaxation. I was so afraid, and there seemed to be no way out of my head or that damn place. If there was anything like hell, this was it! Oh, how much I longed to go to sleep and never wake up again. Oblivion would have been a blessing!

"Until one day I saw someone being taken away in a beam of bright white light piercing the dark grey sky. The sound of gentle, serene music accompanied two female angels who guided the suffering spirit back into the light. From that moment on I started to pray that one day someone would rescue me, too, and bring me to that same place of light. Although I had never prayed in my whole life, and even laughed at people who believed in grace and salvation, I went down on my knees and asked for forgiveness, for compassion, for a new life. I wept more than I knew was possible. My heart was broken into pieces, and I had no hope to putting it back together all by myself.

*The Indomitable Silence*

"Then, one day, my wish was granted. Two beings came out of a stream of brilliant light. This time the color was green. One stepped forward and placed her right hand on my shoulder, gesturing for me to bow my head, which she then cradled with her left hand. Instantly a sense of peace came over me and the screaming voices died away. The angels then carefully laid my fragile body on a stretcher and took me away. Oh, I can still see their warm brown eyes and feel their strong hands carrying me. I closed my eyes and felt the immense power of grace, as a burning flame awoke within me, melting layers of ice around my frozen heart, creating a river of joy right through it. I was saved!"

All this time the old man had been listening breathlessly, the same warm green light glowing gently around him. "Can you take me there, into that light?" he asked, his face now hardly recognizable through the stream of tears running down his face. "There's someone I want to meet!"

"We will, but you've got to be strong. You'll pass through the pieces of your broken heart, and at times you'll wish you hadn't even started your way back home. But you've got to persevere and push through, for the same heart that has been torn apart by the fires of hell can also be touched by the angels in heaven. Come, take my hand. We'll travel fast." The young man reached out his hand, and as soon as the older man took it, the two were gone like a meteor shooting through the night.

I looked around, suddenly brought back to the realization I had been witnessing other people's realities. My eyes met D's. "How long had the old man been here?"

He and his wife strolled the streets for over four years, searching and begging during the day and huddled under old blankets at night, accompanied only by the stars and their unrelenting sadness.

*Tears in Heaven*

When he died his pain deepened, as he was convinced his wife had left him, and the burden of solitude and grief drove him to despair.

"The poor soul."

His illness is that he doesn't know his true nature. We take what we've integrated with us to the other side. Just like going on a trip: we're no more enlightened when the plane lands — until we learn where the bathroom is! Ha ha.

His sudden laughter filled the space around us, and I joined in, thankful for the relief. "I remember Michael saying that one minute before our last breath is basically the same as one minute after. The only difference is we're no longer in a physical body. It's all coming back to me."

That's why it's so important to raise our consciousness and sensitivity while still in a human body. It makes our "landing" over here much easier.

"Where's the old man going now?"

To a place where he can have a good sleep and regain his inner strength. Then his education can start, and he'll realize he has died on Earth and is reborn in spirit. That's the first step. Then he has to learn how to let go of his lower impulses, his compulsive thoughts and emotions. Otherwise he'll continue on like a rudderless boat in a storm, fighting the waves of his shadow, trying not to lose himself in his mind. You want to see?

Before I could answer the question, I was drawn into a dimly lit room where the old man was walking around like a wild animal in a cave, oblivious to the presence of his younger companion, who was standing in the corner. Lost in a red aura of anguish, the man yelled at a photo of his wife: "How could this happen when I needed you most? I'm lost, and now I have nothing!" The man seemed on the verge of a breakdown as he fell on his knees, his face buried in his hands. The scene was heart-wrenching. I breathed deeply. Then the young man walked toward him, crouched down, and put his hand on the old man's heart. He turned his head sidewards and whispered some words in his ear that seemed to calm him down. The bright red around the old man's body changed to soft blue and green, his appearance to one of vigor and vitality. They rose together. "Wow! What happened?" I asked D.

The young man touched his heart just enough to silence his fierce emotions, and to let the tortured thoughts flow out. The old man hasn't yet learned how to do this for himself, but he'll get there. It just takes intention, attention, and practice. Lots of practice.

"Huh! Like anything worthwhile on Earth."

You see, there isn't much difference between the realms.

"Please help me to never lose that focus and self-control." D looked at me with a deep sense of compassion, reached over, and placed a hand on my chest. A rush of warm green light washed around the two of us.

You're already teaching yourself with that request, brother. And I'll be with you every step along the way. Just never stop asking and seeking. Never stop reaching out.

I felt a few tears crawling slowly down my cheek as my attention returned to the scene. "What does the future look like for the old man?"

I don't know, he has free will. He'll likely follow through on his education and enter higher spheres of light, gaining ever more strength and wisdom. It'll take some effort to free himself from his torment, though.

"Was he in hell?"

*Tears in Heaven*

He was in a place he had created himself. The landscape on this side resembles our deepest feelings, and all we experience is an expression of what lives inside. As we live on Earth, so we live in heaven.

"Or hell."

Yes, but neither one is a physical place from which there's no escape. There's always a way out, if there's a will. The intensity of our inner light determines when we're ready to move on. And once we find our way up and taste the beauty of higher love, we never, ever, want to go down again. Only to rescue others, like the young man. Have you noticed how different the old man looks now?

"Yes, much younger, stronger, and full of life!"

You see, it's never too late. No one is forsaken. There's guidance everywhere.

"I would love to do this kind of work here."

It's not the right time.

"You mean I'm not yet ready for *liaison* work?" I was surprised to sense myself smirking cheekily even in this realm. D gave me a sideways glance of annoyance mingled with amusement.

Ha! For you it's still learning time, not serving time. There's a lot more work ahead, I promise. So, you must want to know what happened to the younger man, after he was rescued by his angels?

"Yes, absolutely! I want to see that."

Then set the intention, and...

*The Indomitable Silence*

Next thing I knew, I could see the young man sitting on a bench by the shores of a pristine lake. It was so peaceful and quiet I could even hear his breathing. And I could feel his emotions. Sadness and deep regret for what he had done. Though he had tried to leave drugs and drinking behind, these vices had hijacked his brain and taken him to overdose. How much he missed the ones he had left behind! His wife and daughter, who was only six months old when he had decided to end his life. Then I heard his heart cry. "I'm sorry. I'm so terribly sorry. How could I leave you behind with our little girl? Oh please, forgive me for what I've done."

How he longed to come back and tell his loved ones all that burdened his heart, but he didn't know how. Fortunately, help was near and his deepest wish would soon become reality. I felt myself being lifted, as I went with the young man through a space of faint light. I couldn't see much, but once the air cleared up, we found ourselves descending to street level in a cityscape familiar to him: the restaurant at the corner, the little bookshop beside it, two tiny homes separated by a playground in between, the fountain, and then...

A brilliant light came our way. His home was inviting us in! We floated through the front door and I could see the recognition on his face when he saw everything still looked the same: the hallway, the kitchen table with its four wooden chairs, grandma's old chair, the living room... Home, sweet home. I sensed his heart's longing as he saw his wife sitting on the couch, watching TV. He softly called her name, but there was no response. He tried again, with no response. He shouted; still nothing. He sat down beside her and whispered in her ear and stroked her hair, but it was all in vain.

Grief etched his face as he held her in his arms. How he wished to make contact and tell her he's alive! How he wished to say one more time how much he loved her. He kissed her cheeks and massaged her back and shoulders, which she had always loved. Nothing! She shouted to someone in the other room. His heart throbbed. Then it

*Tears in Heaven*

leapt as a girl came thumping down the stairs. It was his daughter! How much she had grown! She looked around eleven years old.

He jumped off the couch and rushed to her, but he went so fast he ran straight through her. He looked back. She hadn't even noticed. He raised his voice, but also his little girl gave no sign of recognition. He kissed her cheeks and forehead, called her name, pinched her arm, but there was no reaction whatsoever. He stared into her eyes, but she looked right through him.

When he was about to lose himself, an unknown voice came from behind: *"Control yourself, calm your heart."* His spirit master was calling him. *"Do not dwell on your despair. Let your tears of frustration fall away, and connect through your feelings, as it's the only way. Again, be calm, focus on their hearts, and send your love."*

He closed his eyes and it didn't take long before strings of radiant energy connected their hearts, shaping a pyramid of love. It was such a miracle, and I was in the midst of it all! I could see them, feel them, almost touch them. A lump rose in my throat as the daughter sat beside her mum and embraced her. Then the young man gently floated toward them and without speaking or trying to make any physical contact, he spread his arms wide and captured the energy of their love.

His daughter then looked ahead, stood up, walked toward a picture of him and lit a candle, turned off the light, and returned to her mum. The family was together again. This was heavenly grace! I wished the moment would never end, but it soon turned into sadness as I followed the young man upstairs and we stood still before the first room on the left side. The door was locked, concealing the mystery and madness of his last moments. This was where he had ended his earthly life. The desolation on his forlorn face was so poignant and raw that...

*The Indomitable Silence*

As easily as I had come into the scene, I floated back out, leaving the family alone. I was out in the dark, beyond the city, all by myself. I closed my eyes to reflect on what I had just witnessed. When I opened them I saw D was with me again. "That was heartbreaking. I … I don't know what to say."

When the heart breaks, it opens up, softens, and becomes stronger. That's why I brought you here.

"Has he gone back since?"

Yes, many times. He can go on his own now. And what's even more beautiful is that his daughter feels it when he's around.

"What about his wife? Can't she feel him?"

Her sadness is still too strong. But she believes her daughter when she says she feels his presence. It comforts her. She's getting there, slowly.

"That's wonderful!"

Come! There's more I want you to see. Concentrate on me now. We will soon arrive.

I was pulled into a crematory. A coffin stood in the front of the somber space where about twenty people had gathered. I looked closer at the front row. On the left was the woman from the photo in the room where the older man had shouted earlier. Her face was drenched with tears, her eyes puffy and red. Deep grief was buried in her heart. She had lost a great love. Her husband sat next to her, holding her hand, trying to ease her unspeakable suffering. Not only at their son's suicide but also at the pain he must have been going through to take his own life, and the feelings of regret and guilt that they hadn't been able to prevent this heartbreaking end.

*Tears in Heaven*

Then I focused on the right side of the front row. A young woman sat with a baby in her arms. Dressed in black, a veil in front of her face, she was disconsolate. The joy of life had been completely sucked out of her. The baby's crying was soon overlaid and softened by the sweet hum of two angelic beings entering the room from the right. As they stood on either side of the coffin, I looked through my now misty eyes to see a third figure. It was the same young man from the park! He moved near a small table beside the coffin, upon which sat a photograph of him taken at a happier time, during his adolescence.

He moved to the right and stopped in front of the woman and her baby. He went down on his knees and kissed her hand. "I'm sorry, honey," he choked. "I'm so sorry." I could feel his grief, even deeper than his wife's. Then he bent toward the baby and kissed her softly on the forehead. For a moment the child stopped crying and looked around, bewildered by her father's energy.

The young man moved over to the older couple, stood behind them, and laid his hands upon their heads. Regret and sadness seized his heart, but the two angels were sending him love so that he could go on and console his parents, who weren't ready to feel his presence and wouldn't be for years. The older man then turned to look at his distraught wife, and I saw his face. Electricity overtook my entire being, as I recognized him as the old man from the park!

*Do you see?*

D's voice pulled me out of my astonishment and sadness. I stared at him, speechless. He must have seen the mix of puzzlement and realization on my face.

*They are father and son! The young man had finally reached a high enough vibration to start repairing the damage that had sent both his parents into drinking and onto the streets, haunted by shadows of guilt, shame, and indescribable sadness.*

*The Indomitable Silence*

"How is it the old man didn't recognize his son in those other scenes? I knew exactly when I met my grandmother on the other side! There was no doubt whatsoever. I don't understand."

*Each experience is unique. Here the father's grief and confusion kept him at too low a vibration, and the son's frequency was so high that his father couldn't recognize him. Also, the son wanted to wait for a special moment to reveal himself. Speaking of which, let's look in on them again...*

Once again I traveled back in time and found myself in the city park. It wasn't late autumn as I expected, but a sunny spring day. A homeless woman was walking alone on one of the paved paths, looking for food and some human affection. It was the man's wife, still struggling through her daily weariness. The old man broke down, sensing the pain in his wife's heart. Though she was unaware of his presence, he approached her.

"I am here, my love! And I'll never leave you alone!" He turned to the younger man, still unaware of his identity. "Can't you make her hear or see me?" The young man smiled, placed a hand on his father's shoulder, looked toward the woman, and said, "I love you, Mom, and I want you to know Dad is with me now. We are here for you, always."

His mother smiled vaguely, unsure as to why, looked up at the sunlight, and kept shuffling through the park. His father turned to him with a wild look, just as the young man's features changed and softened into something recognizable from happier days. The old man's eyes widened and his jaw dropped. "James?! Is that my little Jimmy? What? How?"

"It's me, Dad! Yes, it's me! I'm so sorry for what I put you two through." His face shone with the wisdom of the heavens and the sweetness of a dove. "But we're together now, and we'll look out for Mom, so she doesn't fall any deeper. Here, love never ends." The two

*Tears in Heaven*

men embraced in an intense glow of blue and green light, weeping with joy. The father kissed his son's face over and over and...

And I was with them, my heart glowing and my body shaking toward an ever higher vibration. D looked at me, smiling reassuringly, and in an instant we were gone from the scene. He spoke to me as we sailed back over the lake.

That's enough strong emotions for now.

"What about the mother?" I looked down and saw the sparkling blue of the lake stretching tens of kilometers through the gentle mountains in either direction. "What happens to her now?"

Soon she'll join them, after a period of cleansing, like her husband. And they both will be there to guide her. She'll be all right. Her faith and will are strong despite all she's been through.

"What a blessing, for all of them!" I found myself wondering about my own path, and my own guides — the ones I had already met and those yet to come. Would I have the inspiration to complete this second book, after the first had challenged me so greatly? Hearing my thoughts, D turned to me and grinned as we soared closer to the shoreline.

You will receive all the inspiration you need, don't worry about that. Your life's path has prepared you. And your angels will never let you down or pass you information that's not clean. You just show up with your heart open to the moment, and hear its whisper in the silence. The book, and more, will come.

Pulled from the air in a burst of light, we were back in the cabin. I was sitting alone at the wooden table. The windows were open, and although it was cool outside, the cabin had stayed warm without a fire on. D was at the small kitchen stove, making some coffee. I gazed at the back of his head, pondering his facial expression. I even mused

*The Indomitable Silence*

that he might turn around and look like Michael, and I would see this was some kind of cosmic joke being played by him all along. But no, when he finally turned around, I saw it was D, smiling and approaching with two mugs, which he set down as he settled into his chair.

Neither of us spoke. We sat quietly, sipping, and enjoying the warm ambiance that swirled with a fresh breeze coming through the windows. Only the sounds of the city and traffic in the far distance intruded into our otherwise silent space. D then pointed to my left, to the pad of paper and a pen. Without hesitation, I put down my mug and took up the writing tools. Beaming with delight, I looked up at him. He grinned and nodded for me to begin. And so I did:

> *I don't know who I am,*
> *and I don't know why I'm here.*
> *I don't know where I come from,*
> *and I don't know where I'm going.*
>
> *But I do know how it feels to be me,*
> *and where my heart has taken me.*
> *And I promise where I'm going,*
> *is where my heart leads me.*
>
> *That's all I need to know,*
> *and that's all I need to do.*
> *The rest is simply not up to me.*
>
> *I am but one dancer in the dance of eternity,*
> *and I'm grateful to be alive.*
> *I don't know who I am,*
> *but I do know who I am in Him.*

*Tears in Heaven*

I turned the page without even thinking about my next words, which flowed onto the paper with such ease and grace, as though guided by a higher power:

> *I am the silence.*
> *No matter the wars in your head.*
> *No matter the clouds in your heart.*
> *No matter the storms in your life.*
> *I am beyond all that.*

> *I am the silence.*
> *I am beyond concern, but I care for you.*
> *I am beyond desire, but I long for your heart.*
> *I am beyond thought, but I dance through your mind.*
> *I am beyond language, but I breathe life into your words.*

I looked up and smiled at those same words — *I am the silence* — affixed to D's wall. I smiled wider now, rolling the pen between my thumb and index finger.

These words are only a beginning.

D's voice now seemed a bit distant, but it refocused my attention on the inside space of the cabin. But when I looked around the cozy room, I saw, once again, he had vanished! Outside perhaps? Without worrying why, and now accustomed to this odd and somewhat annoying tendency of his, I stood up, dropped the pen next to the pad, tore the sheet from the pad, and hurried out into the cool, bright day ahead, folding the paper in my hands as I bounded into the meadow.

~

A crazy sense of urgency carried me down the mountain trail, all the way home, and into the main hall with such speed that I seemed to pass right through the front door. Brimming with excitement, I

*The Indomitable Silence*

shouted hello at the top of my voice, only to find myself standing in an empty house. Everyone was gone. Not even Cinnamon was around.

Exhaling heavily, I took off my coat and boots, shuffled into the living room, and flopped down on the sofa. Would we stay in this house? It was beautiful, but in a few years it would be more than we needed. Also, I still cherished our home in the Netherlands. How would our future look? Many other unanswerable questions came and went. *Embrace the silence*, I thought to myself. Focusing on my breathing, I found my mind going blissfully blank and for quite some time there was nothing, just a feeling of peace and contentment.

The quiet was broken and filled with the energy of daily life, as our back door opened with a *clack* and *swoosh*! In walked Fanny and the girls, and Cinnamon came scampering from behind them and ran toward me. I grabbed him and rubbed his ears vigorously, thinking of D and Glider.

"Hi, Daddy!" the girls chimed, more or less in unison.

"Where have you been all day?" Fanny asked, as she strolled in and placed a few bags on the kitchen counter. It took me a while to respond, as I was still a bit zoned out from my reverie. For a few moments I watched the girls going about their business, unpacking bags, grabbing food, and staring at phones. A wave of pride and gratitude filled my heart.

"Oh, this and that," I finally answered. "Took a hike. Talked to an old guy on the trail."

"An old guy? He must be quite fit, or totally crazy, to be up in the mountains at this time of year," my wife countered with a swiftness and alertness of mind that was so typically hers.

"Yes, he certainly is fit ... and a little crazy, too." I slapped my hands on my knees and pushed off the sofa, and strolled across the living

*Tears in Heaven*

room to the kitchen. I gathered my family in my arms and hugged them with all my might. They looked at me and then at each other, unsure what to make of this sudden burst of manly affection. I simply shrugged, grinned, and sauntered to my favorite room.

Sitting comfortably in my usual soft chair, I turned on the music and the first song of my playlist blasted through the speakers — "The Curtain Falls" by Riverside. How appropriate! I placed the laptop in front of me and dimmed the lights, took out the sheet of paper from my shirt pocket, unfolded it, and placed it beside me for later. It would be part of what I captured about the day.

Soon my fingers were moving with lightning speed, as the fullness of the music enveloped me in its harmonic intention. Though I was aware my hands were moving, I knew the work was being done through me, not just by me. Streams of violet, blue light came from above, and I sensed angelic beings in my periphery, raising my consciousness to a higher vibration. I wrote and wrote, like a madman, until exhaustion overtook me and I fell into a deep sleep.

# THE CITY OF LIGHTS

The light from the countless stars and planets painted a black and white picture in the sky. As we picked up speed, the atmosphere began to brighten like a dawn about to arrive, though I saw no sign of the sun. Soon the intensity was so great that it would have instantly destroyed my retinas were I not outside my earthly body. It was like looking straight into a thousand blazing headlights. The temperature was also surprising, as the otherwise chilly November night had given way to a June-like warmth that pulsated through my entire being. I looked at D. He stared back, smiled, but didn't say a word.

"It feels wonderful here, like a hot bath on the *inside*." Just then a familiar song sounded in my ears. It was "Water of Love" by Dire Straits. "Can you hear that?" Fortunately, he hadn't lost his voice.

Of course, your ears are mine.

"What's going on? Are we in the cabin?"

In a manner of speaking.

"Where are we going?"

No worries, we'll be fine.

"I don't see a radio or speakers. Where's the sound coming from?"

*The City of Lights*

You should know better than to ask questions like this by now. Your physical body is a glove on your spirit one. You don't need physical senses to be conscious, to be aware of your environment, and yourself. That includes seeing and hearing. My gosh, just enjoy the music!

"Okay! Sheesh. You're in a testy mood."

I'm growing a little impatient with your analytical clinging to the material world. You know, you are actually more conscious now, more awake, than you are in your waking state.

"So I'm dreaming?" D shook his head, and I could hear him sigh in exasperation. "Hey look, Mr. Liaison, I'm still a full-on Earthling, I hope, so cut me some slack!"

Well, you're trying, I'll give you that. Sorry I snapped at you.

"Thank you." Awkwardly, neither of us spoke for a bit. "I know you're trying to teach me."

Look, I want to show you what I've experienced when going to heaven, to see Jesus, so I've asked permission to take you into my dreamworld, where we can travel together.

"Oh! Permission?"

Yes, when we want to go somewhere beyond our current power and vibrational ability, we need to ask permission from higher-evolved beings. It's not like "down there," where you can just go anywhere you want — and create some serious havoc!

"Oh right, I remember this from last summer with Michael and Atmos. Are we going to see them again? I would love to say hello."

*The Indomitable Silence*

They are busy dudes. I did speak to them earlier, though, and they told me to say hello and send you their love. But this time, others will greet us. Look, they're here now! Two of your angels.

Two tall, slender light-beings appeared in a haze of soft blue and green. To my surprise, they had no wings, nor were they in long white robes as I had expected. They were dressed like hatless cowgirls with sturdy boots and long jackets, very stylish and hip, and had young, almost childlike, facial expressions. Nodding, the angels spoke to me through my thoughts: *"Hallo, Angelo. Welkom."* I looked at D. He grinned and shrugged.

They know every language, of course. So, why not Dutch-speaking western ladies for your new frontier? Hey, they got tired of the plain white robes and wings. And don't worry about Fanny. Who do you think introduced you to her in the first place? They take their work very seriously, but they need to have some fun, too. Just go with it.

The angels reached out and drew me along with them, and I sensed they had been with me before, like celestial sisters beyond time, aware of every thought and ripple in my heart. The music they summoned was beyond even the most sublime prog rock I had ever listened to, and its glorious sounds seemed to be everywhere.

The sounds are part of a higher realm we're entering. We've left radio Earth behind and are now hearing the first tones of radio heaven. Pretty cool, hey?

"I can't imagine there's even more beautiful music than this."

Oh, there's a lot you can't imagine. But as we travel beyond the land of the human nature, there's plenty that will blow your mind ... so to speak. Ha ha.

*The City of Lights*

Bursting out in the most freeing fit of laughter, we traveled at great speed to destination unknown. The more galaxies of stars flew past us, the more we seemed to stay still, as anywhere became everywhere. Soon we were surrounded and filled with images, as though we *were* the screen of a 4-D movie. We had arrived in D's dreamworld!

Experiences, perceptions, and feelings were all happening within me, and yet from the 360-degree perspective of others as well. But I wasn't the one who could choose which episodes of my life I wanted to watch. They were being chosen for me! And I felt what they had felt, heard what they had heard, and realized how my words and actions, or lack thereof, had affected them.

The first images were of me as a toddler, totally at ease with myself; and of my parents watching me, protective love burning in their hearts. I saw my first love, when I was only five years old, and felt how crushed I was when she didn't want to play with me anymore. Another scene showed me the man who asked my parents to buy me my first tennis racket, and taught me the first principles of the game. His first name, No, was a bit weird, but it was a definite *yes* once I hit my first balls. Then came the face of my favorite coach and how he yearned for my mental and physical improvement when he was being harsh on me. I saw how I had thanked him years later for helping me to forge my discipline, perseverance, and resilience.

The darkness of my post-tennis years then became palpable, as the scenes were clouded in a dark grey fog. I saw my struggle to find some kind of meaning and purpose, and how easy it was to blame others and make excuses rather than to take responsibility for my failures and try harder to make things work. I felt the devastation of dismissal from my first job, as my boss mockingly *praised* me as the worst employee he had ever had. Fortunately, I didn't carry the anger and resentment toward the man for too long. Years of images passed by, accompanied by their associated sounds and emotions. Almost fifty years unfolded in the blink of an eye. There was no sequence

*The Indomitable Silence*

of events, no traveling from place to place. I was in all places, at all times!

Noticeably absent were the things I had considered to be my accomplishments. I saw none of my tennis trophies, nor any of the indicators of the success I had achieved over the fifteen years of running a business. What I did see was how much heart and soul I had put into the work, and how I had treated the people around me. Then I saw the magazine my colleagues presented me on my last day at the helm. It was full of stories and pictures of how they, and some of our best customers, had experienced me. This had been the most valuable, tangible memory of those years, and feeling their love and support filled me with a mixture of deep gratitude and tender melancholy.

My most powerful feelings from recent years came from the help I had received with my first book, *Journey Into the Soul*. I saw all those invisible friends from this realm, inspiring and guiding me, as I tried my hardest to sculpt the book into what I consider the art of my soul. And I felt the ardent hope my creation would connect with others in a deep and meaningful way.

Images of my wife and girls floated by, almost embracing me. Fanny when we first met. Beautiful. The girls when they were born. Adorable, such a gift from heaven. The trips we made and the wonderful memories we shared together, as we grew as a family. Triumphs and challenges. The excitement about our adventure to Canada, and the pride in seeing my girls adapting so well. The many people Fanny had warmly invited into our home. The joy I felt in witnessing these scenes conflicted with my regrets for not spending enough time with them while building my business in Europe, the longing I now felt for going back, and some of my unspoken fears for the future. I let it all run through me; fought none of it. I found myself accepting life's delicious contradictions and confusion. *Let it flow*, I told myself. *Let it flow.*

*The City of Lights*

Certain tough and confrontational moments passed by, some of which I had even forgotten. There was nowhere to hide, no excuses to be made, no one to blame but myself. But it all felt soft and tender. The atmosphere was filled with love, compassion, and understanding. There was no judgment, no condemnation, nor even criticism, except for the moments I could have done better and I knew it.

Clear to me was there's no such thing as an insignificant experience, as even the smallest act can have a profound impact on ourselves, on others, and eventually on the world. But action taken without the heart's involvement will leave nothing of lasting value. The result will be like an artificial tree: pretty in appearance but bearing no fruit. All that matters in the end is how our heart touches that of others, and by doing so awakens the love we all crave.

Then, as quickly as they had entered, the images of the movie were gone, leaving a rich residue of awareness that there was no longer a need to judge myself, prove myself, or compare myself to others; that my true mission was to be the best I can be and shine the light I carry inside, and in doing so bring a bit of heaven to Earth.

*"Turn right! Look!"*

The angel guide on my right had spoken, directing my eyes to something extraordinary hovering in the far distance. The only description even remotely accurate would be to say it was like a giant Christmas ornament hanging in space. As we came closer, the light became more and more intense and the orb grew bigger and bigger, emitting a dazzling array of dancing colors. It possessed an ethereal beauty that filled me with ecstasy.

*"We call it the City of Lights. It's one of the most sacred places you will ever visit."*

*The Indomitable Silence*

It was dazzling! The sky appeared as crystallized gold, quickly changing to blue, white, red, green, and other shades I can't even name. The colors even seemed to respond to our presence, like a welcoming sunrise. But there was no actual sunlight, and time didn't appear to be a linear, one-dimensional experience. Everything seemed to burst out in one glorious instant. "Are there more places as beautiful as this?"

*"There are, but we cannot go there as you are not ready yet. You first have to integrate more love into your being, so your vibration is raised to a higher frequency."*

"This is not God's ultimate home?" I felt a bit disappointed with her explanation.

*"Every place is God's home."*

The angel didn't seem a bit concerned about my disappointment, as she continued.

*"God is the ultimate Source of everything. There's nothing within and beyond time and space, matter and mind, that is not an expression of His infinite, indivisible Being. Let's move on; we have only just arrived."*

We soared farther through the endless golden sky, and after a while my eyes caught a first glimpse of the landscape: a magnificent countryside of lush gardens covered in fragrant flowers, and of tree-covered hillsides; rivers and streams meandering gently through majestic mountain valleys; picturesque villages and streets paved with pure amethyst. Wandering throughout were people of all ages, talking, laughing, and busying themselves with all kinds of fun activities. And in the meadows, animals played and birds sang, celebrating the joy of living. Everything breathed love, pure essence of being. And those colors! Wow! The stunning radiance of the

*The City of Lights*

Northern Lights would have seemed like the mere flicker of a candle in comparison.

*"The fleeting pleasures on Earth are nothing but a shadow of the joy in heaven. Do not think it's a dull place here. It's super entertaining and filled with activity, creativity, and festivity. Nothing is taken away from what you enjoyed before. Here everything is made new in celebration for the Highest."*

The sense of serenity and beauty was so unlike anything I had ever experienced, I had to ask her: "Am I dreaming?"

*"Brother, this is the lost paradise."*

This time it was the angel on my left who had spoken. Her tone was a little rougher and more assertive, though still warm and caring. I looked at her, no longer amused or bemused by the casual rancher clothing. "Lost?"

*"Earth used to be a paradise, created in purity, modelled after this."*

"So it's true we've all lived together in paradise before? And then we fell out of it?"

*"The whole universe is part of God's kingdom. It was when people decided to follow their lower impulses and selfish desires that they lost sight of paradise. They got caught up in distractions, addictions, and obsessions, and walked away from their divine nature. But deep down everyone still has this memory of heaven, and a longing to return. No matter which road you travel, in the end each and every soul will find the way. Heaven can and will wait."*

"And it's never too late?"

*"There's always a way back home, but you have to walk it. No one, not even The One, can do that for you. Others can support you,*

*show you the way, but ultimately you have to walk toward the gates of heaven yourself. And you'll find there are no keys needed to enter, like this City, where there are no walls, no guards, no borders. It's open for everyone."*

"How can we help people get here, so they can see what I'm seeing? This is magical!" My right-hand angel answered this time.

*"The road leads through the heart, as D has been telling you so often. The love awakened there illuminates the path in front of you, so you can see where to go. Knowledge cannot take you there, nor willpower. Only the intensity of light opens the entrance to paradise. Your home here is being prepared by all you do on Earth. Every act of love, every word of encouragement, every thought of compassion, paves the road for your journey here. Even the smallest gesture or good intention has a ripple effect, not only within you but throughout the entire universe."*

"Will we ever recreate this lost paradise?"

*"There's no ultimate, predestined plan written in the sky. It's you, the people, who decide upon that. When there's peace and love in your hearts, there will be peace and love on Earth. Much help and guidance is offered from the higher spheres of light, but we cannot do the work you are supposed to do. So act wisely. The future of your planet is in your hands."*

"Free will. We have free will..." My words trailed off as we neared the City, and I saw buildings much like those on Earth, but flawlessly crisp in conception and construction. Houses, complexes, and meeting halls made of crystallized glass, organized in perfect configurations, all of them filling me with a sense of serenity and certainty that everything was possible here. On the right side impressively large research centers towered high above the streets, flanked by elegant music studios filled with students playing mellifluous melodies my

*The City of Lights*

ears had never heard with instruments my eyes had never seen. On the left were magnificent libraries stacked with countless books, giant theaters with soaring ceilings, and fountains so sublimely ornate as to make Rome's Trevi Fountain seem like a simple spigot.

The temperature was mild, the air fresh and clean with absolutely zero humidity. It felt like one of those sunny days in the Rockies, only with no shade on any mountainside. The light was simply all-compassing. As I basked in this beauty, I saw the multitudes of people, of all backgrounds, coming and going on paths between the buildings, clearly having fun playing and being creative. Bliss filled me as I longed to connect with these beautiful souls. But none of them seemed to be talking.

Heart talk!

I never would have expected to flinch in heaven, but I did. I turned my head and looked backwards. D was speaking as he approached, but like my angel sisters, his lips weren't moving.

Ladies! Nice to see you here again. I trust you're having a good "workday."

All three of them laughed gregariously. D was right: the other realm is a little surreal. Hearing angels laugh was a strange yet thrilling experience, like music beyond music. Then I saw how a stream of warm green light connected their hearts, and I sensed it reaching toward me too. I looked down and surrendered, letting it wash over me. D continued.

Here we don't need words to communicate, as there isn't any space between what we think, say, and feel. The heart talks! I'm still learning this art, even as a liaison. And when I'm out of line, your two sisters here don't hesitate to let me know. With love, mind you.

*The Indomitable Silence*

The rougher angel sister laughed a little teasingly at his comment. D made a face, and the three of them chuckled again. I smiled and looked over at the City. Then, as D had advised me to do, I let silent words flow from my heart, and it worked! "I would love to communicate this directly on Earth."

You can! Nestle into the center of your heart and you'll hear the falling of a dead leaf, the whisper of a long lost friend, and the voice of love guiding you. Then you'll hear...

"The silence! Just like in..."

My cabin, that's right! I got those words from here. God awakens in the heart and whispers His unspoken words once the mind is silent. Your truth, His truth.

"Oh, right. Uh..."

Don't worry, you're not judged with fire. It's more like looking into a pristine mirror you can't lie to. Deep down you know when you've done something good and when not. And you've done both, as we all have. You want to see some of it?

"Um... Aren't we supposed to meet Jesus?"

Be patient! See, that's me yelling at you with love. You wanted to know how to connect, so I'm going to show you. Let's go.

D pointed out a path leading toward a stream up ahead, and we made our way toward it. Nowhere did I see a single dead blade of grass or a wilting flower petal. Vibrant light filled everything, creating a translucent garden beyond the most beautiful I had ever seen. I looked back to see if we had left any footprints on the grass, but saw none. We continued on for a short while. When we arrived at the stream, I stared down and saw water so crystal clear I could see the

*The City of Lights*

twinkling in my eyes staring back at me. I knelt down, took some in my cupped hands, and drank. Its coolness refreshed my entire body.

This is the river of life. Jump in!

"Jump in?"

Oh, come on. Don't be a wimp, just jump.

The narrow river looked shallow, but nevertheless I took a short run and leapt. The moment my body touched the water its level rose, keeping my feet from touching bottom. First my hips, next my arms, and then my neck slipped beneath the surface, leaving only my head above as I floated for a few moments. And then it happened. The water pulled me completely under. However, before I had time to panic, I was filled with the buoying realization that I would not drown. How was this possible?! As quickly as the question arose I was back on the shore, standing on the grass, completely dry. D was smiling, but soon his face turned serious.

This is a very special river, as you've probably noticed. This one doesn't take lives, it gives eternal life.

We stared at each other, feeling the crisp breeze as it rushed between the buildings and across the open lawn where we stood. Then, as though I were expecting it, D leaned in close to me with an impish grin and continued.

Water doesn't only heal wounds, it wipes away fear and sadness, too. That's why Michael had you pushed into that pool in Spain when you were a little boy. I've seen the footage. Solid spiritual work, I must say. A classic approach!

My two guides nodded in agreement. I looked at D. "Oh? Is that so? Then I should be thankful, I guess." My friend winked and motioned his head in the direction of the path.

*The Indomitable Silence*

Let's move on.

D turned toward a cluster of buildings a little farther along the river and walked in that direction. My two angel sisters floated somewhere out of sight, and yet I knew they would be at my side in a flash if necesarry. As we made our way toward what looked like a university, I felt myself relaxing into the experience while people moved toward us, smiling, their whole beings connected to us by the same warm green light. I was really starting to love that hue! Their faces looked vaguely familiar, like when you run into a bunch of people who look like they could have gone to high school with you in a parallel universe. It was that same effect, and although I didn't care much for schools, the camaraderie here was instantaneous and unmistakable. We all smiled at each other, I somewhat cautiously.

These are souls who are drawn to our vibration. This is recognition, brother, in the same way you can tell someone you meet at a party is going to be a lifelong friend. And there are more than just friends here.

I gave D a questioning look, but he just grinned as we moved on, silently looking around us, until suddenly he halted. "Why do you stop?" I sensed palpable waves of anticipation running through him.

Wait here, okay? I'll wave when it's time.

He moved stealthily, as if to catch someone by surprise. My vision became rather blurred, and all I could see were three figures. Then one of them turned, and they all started running toward him. They embraced with such love that it was clear to me I was witnessing a family reunion. These three were his wife and two kids! The singular beauty and emotion of the moment made me think of my own family, and how much I missed them now. As I breathed in deeply, I saw him wave. Then, out of nowhere, my heart heard the one word that can enter me with no resistance at all—

*The City of Lights*

"Daddy!"

Did I hear that right? I moved forward with a single thought, and then heard it again, but it was another girl's voice—

"Daddy!"

My vision cleared as two children, one a little taller than the other, came running toward me, their arms outstretched and their feet off the ground. My eyes widened and my arms opened as my own daughters jumped into my arms and knocked me to the ground! But, how?! Joy was soon overtaken by dread, as I puzzled at why my girls were here in heaven. "Are they…?"

Don't forget you're in my dreamworld.

"What? So have I taken your place?"

I've let you in to experience my dream, but it's your version of it! This happens all the time here.

"But how…?"

Listen, you can experience what others do, how they think and feel, but it's always seen through your eyes and felt through your heart. This is how you can connect more deeply. You'll see.

My girls had finally let go of me and I was able to get up on my feet again. I wanted to ask them how they could be in heaven while still living with me under the same roof on Earth, but fear was holding me back. How can you ask your own children if they are dead? I felt myself spinning in confusion. D must have sensed this and put my worries to rest.

Heaven is not for the dead, it's for those who are truly ALIVE.

*The Indomitable Silence*

"Did you eat from the trees yet, Dad?" my eldest, Chiara, interrupted with that disarming expression of hers I had come to know so well. "The fruit here is delicious! No pesticides or pollution. It's heaven for a vegetarian like me!"

"Oh! No, not yet. You mean you've been—?"

"Dad, all this time here and you still haven't tried?" Alyssa asked incredulously.

"Even better than Mom's food!" Chiara piped in. "Though don't tell her that. I mean, it's hard to compete with this. Here—" She tossed me an extra apple she was carrying, and I snatched it, surprised at how little effort it took.

"Thank you. But what are you girls talking about? I've just arrived here. What do you expect?"

"No, we've been here together many times, Dad. Oh, come on!" Alyssa insisted, with wide eyes that betrayed her disappointment. "I can't believe you don't remember."

"I'm sorry, but I don't!" I replied, feeling a little annoyed by her boldness. "I'm not dead yet, young lady." *Am I?* I wondered, forgetting that thoughts can be read here. I rolled the apple between my fingers, trying to get a handle on what was happening.

"But you don't need to die first," Alyssa said. "Actually, we're here quite often. When we're asleep, we come here and have a good time. You too, Dad!" What was she telling me? That we visit heaven while asleep at night? And we often came here together? I felt a bit frustrated I couldn't remember any of this. I turned to D.

"You said I wasn't dreaming!"

*The City of Lights*

As I was starting to say, you're now seeing your daughters' dreamworld. They are young and the innocent belief in magic is still close to their hearts, though they don't remember having been here when they wake up. But you, like most adults, have lost that connection with the magical realm, because you're too busy in your head. Your girls see you now struggling to remember, and so of course they're teasing you. Daughters — cheeky even in heaven!

"Indeed!" I looked at my girls quizzically, before turning to D. "And how is it you are connected then?"

Really, you ask this? Besides it being part of my liaison role, by my age you'll learn to be as a child again. And I like having a good time. Hey, what's wrong with that? An old man should make the best of his remaining days, right?

"It seems to me you'll have all the time in the world here."

Here is Now, brother. Here is Now. There is no tomorrow. There is no time. At least, not as you understand it.

Not at all concerned about our little intermezzo, Alyssa continued pressing the matter, as she often does when she's bothered by, or curious about, something. Once again I said I didn't recall, but I assured her I would surely remember this time. Somewhat satisfied, she gave me a hug and apologized for the sharp tone she had taken with me. "That's okay, sweetie. I know you're just trying to share something special."

Happy, I stood back and beheld my lovely daughters, pondering D's questions and the humbling challenges of fatherhood. Clarity, I now realized, could only be found in the present moment, and so I turned my attention to the apple. To my amazement, it was perfectly formed, without any blemish or rough spot, and the range of reds seemed to shift across a stunning spectrum before my eyes.

*The Indomitable Silence*

"Try it, Dad!" Chiara urged me. "You'll see what I mean."

Slowly, I lifted the fruit and took a bite. What I experienced almost defies description. The essence was so pure I sensed its nourishment becoming one with my entire being even as I swallowed! And the aliveness and freshness now surging within me seemed connected to the eternal intelligence of all things. Astonished, I looked at the girls and then at D. We smiled at each other with contented knowingness, as Alyssa called—

"Look, Dad!" She proudly displayed her ability to lift herself from the ground and hover above a few trees in a nearby park next to a path. "I can fly! It's so freeing to be here, really cool. And they've got some really fun games, too. I don't miss my iPad at all!"

Her innocence and playfulness were even more charming here. I smiled, and then noticed Chiara looking intently at both of us. She spoke. "Okay, Dad, we're going now. We have other stuff to do. And don't you dare follow us! See you later." In a flash she was in the air with her sister, and then the two vanished. Though they were gone, I still felt their presence in my heart. A warmth I knew would never leave me. I looked at D. My longing for more time with them was clear to him.

Something, hey? But you were getting too emotional. Your vibration isn't high enough to withstand such intense experiences for too long. There's a learning curve to this. You'll get there, don't worry.

We made our way to the path near the trees, and then continued in silence for several moments. Typical of me, my thoughts soon turned to the practical. "Do people ever work here?"

You think this is La La Land? It would be boring to just loaf around and do nothing! No, we want to use our skills, our talents, our

*The City of Lights*

passions. They were given for a reason. And we want to play, have fun! That's what life is all about. It's a play, a dance, that never ends. Oh, and get this! You know those times when you're writing and you feel that warm, tingling presence? That's your two angel sisters coming to your aid, to channel inspiration from heaven and guide you in your craft. Amazing, isn't it?

Curious, I peered around to see where they were. As I had hoped, they reappeared nearby, smiling and waving. But when I smiled back, they sped off again. I cast a querulous glance at D. All he did was grin. I was not amused, but he looked like he couldn't care less.

Look!

A short distance from the path was a semi-enclosed work area, like the service bay of a garage. To one side sat a small structure, which appeared to be an almost-finished project. Looking more closely, I felt myself tingling from feet to head, as I realized it was D's cabin! "That's your shack!"

Ha! Yes, all designs start here in these studios of inspiration. In my dreams, I came here to work, and once I figured it all out, I started building my little haven on the mountainside. Nice, hey?

"Not to sound selfish, but did you build one for me too?"

I already did, and then I invited you. Like the character Ray in the movie Field of Dreams, I didn't question it. But instead of building a baseball diamond in an Iowa cornfield, I built a cabin on a rocky outcrop in British Columbia.

We grinned at each other. "And now you're *easing my pain*, as the voice says to Ray in the movie?"

Well, how am I doing so far? That was a rhetorical question, by the way. I know exactly how I'm doing, because—

120

*The Indomitable Silence*

"You can see everything more clearly here in heaven, so…" I paused, gripped by a question that should have been obvious to me earlier. "Does Fanny ever come here?" D became unusually quiet, looking down as we walked along the path between some more buildings.

You two have somewhat different views on spirituality. But I want you to know something.

"Yes?" I could see his expression turn to one of excitement, as though he were concealing a secret about a surprise party.

None of that matters here! Only love does. Now, are you ready to see the man who brought the biggest dream to Earth?

Before I could ask him more about my wife, my two guides were on either side of me, their arms locked in mine as the four of us entered a square where a large crowd had gathered. A podium had been built at the far end, and we made our way through the vast rows of people. The ambiance was electrifying. Was this the moment I had been waiting for?

Look closely now. It's about to start.

I had read a lot about Jesus and loved his teachings, but I had always considered a personal connection to be a far-off experience, out of reach. For me it was hard to feel the intimacy of a relationship with someone I had never met. That was about to change.

Be still in your heart. This is how to listen.

I heard what D said, but was too emotional to be still. A sheer burst of joy and excitement shot through me, almost too much for my mind to bear and my heart to hold. What would he be like? And would I be able to look into his eyes, even from this distance? I felt faint, but my angels were at my side. They winked knowingly. I giggled nervously,

*The City of Lights*

like a child not knowing what to expect. With a soft voice, D gave me another instruction.

Focus on his presence and you'll be as close as you can be.

"Are all these people Christians?" I whispered, thinking of the people in our church community.

Shh. Here it's not about what you believe, but about what lives in your heart. When Jesus said he was the way, he meant the path is available to everyone — through the heart.

A big roar went through the crowd. I fixed my eyes on the podium, but didn't see anything. Anticipation slowly gave way to confusion when the cheering became louder and louder, and yet there was no sign of anyone on the stage. Then it hit me: Jesus was not going to be there; he would stay on the ground, among the people! My eyes scanned the environment, but still couldn't detect any sign of his coming. Then, seemingly out of the blue, he manifested himself on the spot, and there he was, no more than six feet away, with people buzzing around him like bees on a flower, eager to get their nectar.

All of a sudden the sounds died, and he was right in front of me. The crowd seemed to have vanished into oblivion as it was just the two of us. Oddly, his appearance bore none of the expected features: no beard, no robe, no stigmata… In fact, I cannot describe what he was wearing, as a pure light emanated from his body, the color of which kept changing like a prism. I wasn't looking at him so much as I was feeling him in my heart. His joy was my joy. His peace was my peace. And I hung my head in humility in the presence of a being who channeled God's truth so perfectly, without any sign of misplaced self-importance. My identity washed away as his thoughts came to me directly: *"Raise your head. Do not fear my eyes. Do not fear…"*

*The Indomitable Silence*

My heart pulsing, I mustered up all my courage and raised my head until our eyes met. Love of unfathomable depth fell upon me. His eyes shone like gems of turquoise, and his stare was so mesmerizing I instantly knew he could read everything written in my heart, every ache and hope. Yet there was no judgment, only compassion. In that very moment I realized Jesus saw the light in me, no matter what I thought of myself. And I knew he wanted me to see myself and others likewise. A million questions swirled around in my head, but his presence was enough to answer them all. A sense of knowing arose beyond earthly understanding. I pinched myself. Was this nothing but a dream? No, I was standing face-to-face with the living Light of the World!

*"You are like a son to me. Trouble your mind no longer as you go about your days. You are free in me."*

I fell to my knees and sobbed. My angel sisters crouched beside me and put their arms around me. D squatted in front of me and looked around, as happy and casual as a concertgoer at an outdoor festival. He then spun on his heels, cupped my face in his hands, and gave me an encouraging nod. Soon my legs gathered strength and I rose to my feet.

*"I am with you. Meet me in your heart. That's where the kingdom is. Meet others in the same sacred space. That is the way. Start with those who brought you here."*

I looked at D, we joined hands, and Jesus's words spread out among the people as they sighed and swayed in reverence.

*"Dear brothers and sisters, I am happy to see all of you here. Give thanks and know it is your heavenly Father's greatest desire to see everyone united in His eternal Light. Until that glorious day your work will call you, to raise the love and consciousness in this universe.*

*The City of Lights*

*"Open your hearts fully and embrace the light that is your true identity, and then walk among others with your eyes wide open to see where your hands may serve. All good deeds, no matter how small, are remembered in heaven, as what you do to your brothers and sisters you do unto me.*

*"When you see the homeless begging for money, what do you see when you look in their eyes? Do you see their true nature? Do you see me? For I am there, in the depth of everyone's heart, and when you walk away from that sacred space, you walk away from me. Speak with kindness, act with compassion, care for the weakest, and you will honor me.*

*"Use your talents, but take no credit for your work, for everything is given by the Highest. Follow your passions, but make sure you also use them for the benefit of others, for all you give will find its way back to you. Lend your shoulders, carry those whose legs fail them, and guide those whose vision is blurred by the fog of pain and selfishness.*

*"Ask yourself, what have you done with the life you were given? Have you done your work the best you could, and by doing so served God to the best of your abilities? Do not be seduced by wealth, for the earthly material is but a tool; do not make it your focus or your ultimate goal. That path leads only to darkness and loneliness, away from Him, from me, from your soul.*

*"The way to the kingdom is through the light of love that brightens the darkness and restores faith and hope. Stay in that space, and never forget my words, for they will guide you if you get lost along the way. Walk as far as you can go, but remember the way back to me is through a church not made with hands. You are God's children, you are blessed, and I am with you. Always."*

*The Indomitable Silence*

After these final words, he disappeared into the crowd, which was now awash in bright white light revealing every blissful face, each soul ready to cherish eternal life and embrace the mission to serve. Soon the light grew so blinding that everyone's individuality seemed to dissolve, and I could feel we were all one! I felt complete and pure, as if his presence had cleansed my soul of all impurity. But I knew that I was not to stay still, that more work was to be done, that I must keep moving. The gentler of my two angels then spoke.

*"One day you will fully have realized what you just heard, and this land will be yours to walk. Now come, there is more to show you."*

I felt the pull of my angels, who clearly wanted to draw my attention to the edge of the crowd. My chest rose and I swallowed hard. My spirit was heavy and light at the same time, as my feet froze to the ground below me. It was her! I stepped forward from my companions to get a closer look at my wife. She was wandering peacefully by herself, happy with her usual sense of joy and lightness, looking for something to attend to.

As the sound of her name passed through me, she looked over and smiled before walking into a nearby building. My feet unlocked from where I was standing, simply by the intention of my heart. I followed her into what looked like a sort of discotheque. Soon it hit me what was happening. This was the place where we had first met in Indonesia so many years earlier! But only in essence, for the particulars were different. The doors opened and I entered the rich blue glow of the dance floor, where she now twirled to thumping dance music beneath the sparkling lights in which she looked even more enchanting.

She stopped spinning, turned to face me, and began swaying to the music as I approached. Taking her in my arms, we moved to the rhythm of the sounds in our heart, speaking with our eyes, which seemed to summon our shared memories and project them into the

*The City of Lights*

space between us. The stream of images had an odd density about it, which bound us while holding us slightly apart. Though apparently in heaven, my earthly concerns returned in ways more clear to me now. Would we all stay together in Canada? And how would the preferences of our children take shape in the decisions to come? We stopped dancing and I looked intently into her eyes. "You know I want the best for our family. You understand my quest, don't you?"

Pulling me close to her, she kissed me lovingly and squeezed me in her arms. She then took me by the hand and led me to a far door I hadn't noticed before. With an inscrutable grin on her face and a tender caress on my cheek, she opened it and guided me through, softly closing it behind me. And then...

I was in the entertainment room of our house! At least it looked like it, with the exception of the lighting, which now had a turquoise radiance much like those lovely eyes I had looked into earlier. Slowly touching the furniture, walls, and shelves, I stepped down to my usual chair in front of the large screen and settled in to see what would happen. Music was already bursting forth from the speakers, but it was a little different from my usual selection. The bass vibrations of the music were matching frequencies deep within. I closed my eyes and let the sounds wash over me awhile, until the screen turned on by itself and flooded the room with bright green light, revealing images of times where my heart had taken a picture. There were many, but three in particular stood out.

I saw an old friend of mine, Paul, whom I had helped by setting him up in a new home when he was going through some hard times. He smiled at me, and I could feel his lonely heart beating with a joy that had been hidden for too many years. What amazed me was that just witnessing this scene created an even stronger reaction in me than it had done more than twenty-five years earlier. This warm feeling stayed with me for the duration of the entire movie.

*The Indomitable Silence*

Next there was a homeless man in a wheelchair playing his harmonica near Kelowna's waterfront. I sat beside him as he offered me life story snippets. Diagnosed with cancer a few years earlier, and without a home or family, he made the best of his remaining days by bringing joy to passersby through his music. I was deeply moved to see how happy he was, despite his abject life conditions, and how he was a sparkling light for others. His lesson to me was even more of a blessing than I realized at the time.

Then I saw a family with three kids we had helped not long before, when life hit them with a thunder ball. She was battling with cancer while they all were grieving the recent loss of a newborn child. It was too much for a human heart to bear. And it seemed a small thing to help them escape the hardship of life even for a few days, and pay for their vacation at a family resort near Amsterdam. To see all of them smile was more than my heart could have asked for. As I was watching many other scenes, the blessing of being able to come to the aid of those in need caressed me like a clean wind of truth. I felt grateful.

You see how good it makes you feel to help people, and bring a smile to their face? Starting to see a pattern for future choices?

I turned to see D sitting at the far-end seat to my left, still beaming from the heavenly speech earlier. He clasped his hands on his belly and tilted his head to await my reaction. I found myself grinning at the realization this man must be an angel packaged in an old fragile human body. "How the heck did you get into my inner sanctum?!"

Ha ha! Well, first, you know I have skills you're still discovering. Second of all, I got tired of waiting for an invitation. After all, you've been to my place many times. Sheesh! Thirdly, are you so sure we're in your home?

"I know, we're still in heaven, aren't we?"

*The City of Lights*

Where is heaven?

"Oh, you mean all of this is still happening in your cabin?" My friend unclasped his hands, braced himself on the plush seat, and leaned toward me intently. His face became dead serious.

My friend, you are ALWAYS in the cabin when you live from the heart.

Before I could ask him to elaborate, the green light expanded and filled the entire space like a mist, obscuring my friend, though I could sense he was still smiling. Surrendering to the sudden levity of the moment and the exhaustion of the day, I let the drowsiness overcome me and slipped into a blissful sleep.

~

I awoke later, with no idea how much time had passed. I was still in my entertainment room, which now seemed as it always had. The screen was on but it was blank, and the music was no longer playing. All was quiet, except for the sound of Fanny and the girls chatting, laughing, and preparing food in the kitchen. Rubbing my face, I sat up and looked around. To my side sat my open laptop. Curious, I picked it up and looked at the screen. To my delight, I saw fresh words added to my growing passage:

*I am the silence.*
*No matter the wars in your head.*
*No matter the clouds in your heart.*
*No matter the storms in your life.*
*I am beyond all that.*

*The Indomitable Silence*

*I am the silence.*
*I am beyond concern, but I care for you.*
*I am beyond desire, but I long for your heart.*
*I am beyond thought, but I dance through your mind.*
*I am beyond language, but I breathe life into your words.*

*I am the silence.*
*I am the joy in your smile.*
*I am the sadness in your tears.*
*I am the whisper in your stillness.*
*I am the love in your courage.*

# THE INDOMITABLE SILENCE

David had been crying all night when he felt a gentle touch on his skin. More than this, it was the voice that had shaken him to his core: *"All is well. Have faith in Me and you will see the light, and the way."* Near rock bottom, he was aware of a divine presence for the first time in his life, despite all the cynicism and frustration that had characterized his world.

As he shared with me this life-changing experience of the previous May, his eyes were tearful, as were mine. Though I had seen him in church a couple of times, we had never really gotten to know each other. All I knew was that he wasn't from a Christian family and that his path had been one marked by some staggering highs as well as some heartbreaking lows. He told me that he had been a successful contractor, and a caring husband and father, until the burdens of work and family life sank into the dark side of his heart, propelling him into the coping fallacy of drugs and alcohol. He lost himself, his wife and children, and eventually his home. Maybe worst of all, he lost his dignity. David slipped into the dark night of the soul, and then onto the streets.

More than once he planned to end it all and disappear into oblivion, but through many highly unlikely coincidences he stayed alive. Each time he was on the verge of taking his life, someone showed up and stopped him. Once, the police even closed down part of a highway bridge, after passing motorists saw him standing on the edge and

*The Indomitable Silence*

called 911. Eventually, after years of David suffering with addiction, his sister reached out and pulled him from the precipice, and took him in.

And now, we were all taking him in, here on a sunny Sunday of a family camping weekend at Green Bay Bible Camp in Kelowna. It was a stunning spot near the lake and we were blessed with gorgeous weather. The kids were playing games and doing all kinds of fun activities in and out of the water, while the adults spent their time sharing stories and enjoying the majestic beauty of the valley scenery. After telling me his heartfelt tale, David shone with a sense of hope and faith, as he prepared for his baptism.

When he passed by the people who had gathered on the beach, and walked into the lake toward Pastor Mike, David looked like a proud groom, with the exception of his white shorts, which were delightfully out of place. But there was no sense of incongruity when he went under the water and then emerged with a scream of liberation from the bottom of his heart, now overflowing with joy. After hugging his sister, he walked over to me and we embraced each other firmly, knowing the old David was no more; he was reborn. He had found God in the deepest pain of his soul, and his life would no longer be the same. And I had found a friend whose story would live forever in my heart.

A few months later David suffered cardiac failure and died instantly. Apparently the years of substance abuse had taken their toll on his fragile body. Sad though the news was, those of us who had come to know the man were grateful he had opened his heart, found peace, and shared some of his soul with us. His final resting place was therefore not in the earth but in the hearts of those who had been touched by his light. Fortunately, I was one of them. "So long, brother," I said to myself the moment I heard of his passing, "We will meet again."

*The Indomitable Silence*

Glider's barking outside pulled me out of my daydream. I looked around and saw D nodding to me over the usual mugs and plates on the table. He stood up and walked to the open window, curious as to what was provoking his furry little buddy. We were in the cabin, though I had forgotten coming here, so engrossed was I in David's story. D had been listening to my thoughts.

Each time we lose someone we love, they nestle in a special place in our heart, while the void left behind seems impossible to fill.

"It's strange but although I didn't know him that well, I really miss him. He was an unpolished diamond: rough on the outside and pristine on the inside. I wanted to become closer friends, yet time decided differently." Glider was still barking, but D ignored him for the time being, not wanting to lose his thread of heart's thoughts.

What is opened is always more important than what is broken. David had tried to fill the emptiness and pain with drugs and alcohol. Of course, in vain. But the moment he surrendered, in all his brokenness, his heart opened its windows, which gave the pain a way out and the light a way in.

I nodded silently, but I found myself more distracted by the dog than D was. "Is everything okay out there?"

Oh, I think he's still upset we didn't take him on our heavenly trip. He's just a dog, you may think, but he sensed my absence. And he knows other animals are there, playing and having tons of fun, so maybe he's not so pleased about that. I'll take him next time.

Apparently reassured by his master's promise, Glider turned silent. And my thoughts returned to David, bringing back a sense of sadness and emptiness. "Who would have guessed he had such battles brewing in his lonely heart back when he seemed on top of the world? And then when he lost it all, the darkness he must have felt… We judge

*The Indomitable Silence*

the rich and the poor differently, but the heart and soul are beyond such prejudices, aren't they? Loneliness knows no tax brackets." D grinned knowingly and leaned forward on his elbows, staring at me for several moments before speaking.

After my loved ones died, the grief and emptiness were beyond bearable. That dark night of the soul, as your friend had to go through, felt like the only place I would ever live again. But I managed to hang on. After most of my tears had been shed and I felt completely dried up inside, I decided to remake my life with complete simplicity. I gave up my business, my house, my car, my computer, my TV. Most of my money and possessions went to charities and a few close friends who needed it more than I did. Matter no longer mattered to me. I built the cabin. This, and Glider, are everything to me. This is the only home I need. This is my last mountain!

His eyes were telling tales of sadness and gratitude, as he continued in a whispering tone.

When something is taken away, it's good to look for what has been given in return. Since the day I lost my three earthly angels, three heavenly ones have been watching over me. I don't want bitterness and grief to be my last footprints. I know my loved ones are just a dream away, and I want them to be proud of me! In fact...

He leaned back and looked upward, and I heard his heavy breathing. As he lowered his head and his gaze met mine, I saw a curious sparkle in his eyes. He took a sip from what was left in his coffee mug, set it down with a woody thud, and stood up. His swift movement surprised me, but I let it be. There was something he wanted me to see.

Let's go.

*The Indomitable Silence*

Out we went, but this time we took a different trail, one to the left of the rocky outcrop. Glider scampered ahead, as though he could read his master's mind and was in on some secret plan. The day was sunny and warm, so I enjoyed the walk along this new path. Anticipation stirred in me when I saw a plateau meadow appear. How had I not seen all these nearby spots in the few years we had lived here?

D slowed down and whistled loudly to Glider, who stopped and waited for us near what looked like crosses in the ground. My heart became heavy with dread as D knelt in front of them, took a little note from his jacket pocket and laid it against the first cross. Putting a small rock on it, he looked up and saw the horror and sadness on my face.

They're not actually buried here. It just gives me a place to visit, a reminder of our love. And when I want to share what's in my heart, I leave them a note like this. I know I can always pray and be with them that way, but ... I like notes.

"The actions of the hands give us a visual of the heart." D smiled sadly, nodded in agreement, and shakily pushed on one knee to stand up. I reached out my hand to help him and felt him trembling. He hadn't been this frail since our first meeting. I put my arm around him as we made our way to a nearby log and sat down in silence for quite a while.

People say we don't regret the things we've done, only those we haven't. I don't know if that's always true, but I do know I regret the kisses I didn't give, the laughter I didn't share, and the tears I didn't wipe away.

He paused for a moment, lost in thought. I could feel the rawness of his emotions and how close they were under his skin. I felt them deep in my heart.

*The Indomitable Silence*

I used to think success is about the mountains we climb and the summits we reach. Now I know it's not. It's about the people who are with us when we rise, when we rest, and when we fall. The real treasures are not what we've accumulated, but the ones in our heart.

Again I was stunned by the sprinkles of wisdom that followed the downpour of his heart's cry, as though he pushed a button that enabled him to switch from one mode to the other in a split second. His contrasts were fascinating; so human, yet so spiritually enlightened; so fragile, yet so strong; so vulnerable, yet solid as a rock. He was a tremendous inspiration, a beacon of light. "D, you remind me of someone I met not so long ago. But it's a long story."

Ah! Well, share away. We have nowhere to go. And, as I'm sure you've surmised by now, I see time a little differently than many. Ha ha.

It was great to hear him back to his laughing self. "Well, I saw her for the first time sitting in a chair for disabled people, listening to one of the lecturers. We were on a fourteen-day Mediterranean cruise, Israel being the main attraction. The trip was organized by Hay House, a major publisher in the field of self-help and spirituality, and Dr. Wayne Dyer was the main reason why many people had signed up. However, two weeks before our embarking in Rome, Wayne passed away in his sleep at the age of seventy-five. I was so disappointed, as he was one of the few people who had inspired me with his books and teachings.

"Finding the three replacement speakers flat-out boring, I felt a bit deflated, regretting the money I had spent. Until I met her. She was an elderly German lady whose eyesight had suddenly started to deteriorate eleven years earlier, leaving her visual world one of only faint shadows of colors, until ultimately everything went black. Despite her blindness, she had signed up for the cruise to the holy

*The Indomitable Silence*

land, traveling all the way by herself from Australia. At one point, I told her I thought she was very brave. She shook her head, smiled, and said she was just a little crazy. I found her lively sense of humor an inspiring triumph over her struggles.

"She was alone most of the time. Alone at breakfast, after a staff-member would wheel her from her cabin to the restaurant. Alone during daytime on the deck, when most passengers spent time with their families or engaged in all kinds of activities. Alone at dinner, where every evening she sat in the same spot. And alone at night, when her dreams were her only company. I guess most of us focused mainly on her blindness, if we saw her at all. But she could see so much more than we did. Through her heart she saw past what we only perceived with our eyes or assumed in our minds.

"The first time we met was quite an unusual experience. As I took the empty seat beside her at the back of the theater, she turned toward me and, without a word, put her hand on mine. She told me her name was Andrea and that I had come at exactly the right moment. Intrigued, I asked what she meant by that. She just smirked and said she needed to go to the washroom. Chuckling, I guided her. After we had returned to our seats, she took my hand again and didn't let go for quite some time. It was awkward at first, as I'm not used to holding hands with someone I hardly know. But she was different. I felt at ease with her, familiar, and I'm sure she must have felt the same way.

"She told me there had been times in her life when she didn't feel comfortable at all with herself. She had suffered severe depression both before and after her sudden blindness. For many years she believed happiness wasn't something she would ever find again. She had searched for it everywhere; in relationships, in other countries, in expensive vacations, in a beautiful home. However, it had always eluded her, until she was so tired that she stopped her pursuit. And that's when happiness found her! She had been chasing something that was only waiting for her to turn inward and become still.

*The Indomitable Silence*

"The biggest takeaway for me was her explanation that life isn't supposed to make us happy. She said the way we experience life depends for the most part on the story we tell ourselves about it. Can we accept life as it is with all its quirky twists and turns, without believing or even wishing it should be different, or do we resist life and talk ourselves into a continual state of dissatisfaction and frustration? Every challenge offers the opportunity to build us up, yet at the same time involves the danger of degrading us. If we truly realize this, she said, we can use every moment as an opportunity to become more heart-centered, leaving only the real challenges as doorways to awakening, rather than imaginary ones that close doors in our faces."

Some precious jewels from a wise lady.

"We are all enrolled in the never-ending journey through life, a quest for our truth, and we learn lessons whether we like them or not. They come back in various forms, and not until we have mastered them will we move on to the next level. We are apt to make mistakes, but every failure bears the seed of growth, especially the ones that hurt the most. Everything we need to succeed will be given: talents, strengths, opportunities, circumstances, the right people. But we must do our part to move forward, right now.

"Never make *there* your *here*, she said. See what's in front of you, even if it's not what you're looking or hoping for. Embrace the work at hand, even if it's not exactly your first choice. Don't be a prisoner of your likes and dislikes. Do what's needed and do your best. That's all you can do. The rest is simply not up to you." D nodded silently and humbly bowed his head, giving her words even more dignity. "You're not saying much."

Too many words can be the mark of a fool, while the right ones can knock down the walls around the heart and light a path right through it. She nailed it, though!

*The Indomitable Silence*

"I know I was meant to meet her. A cruise I had regarded as a waste of time and money ended up offering me the opportunity to shift my perspective, as I experienced on this mountain when you first took me to the cabin. By the way, she also gave me a splendid definition of happiness."

I'm all ears...

"Happiness is peace in motion."

Like the sunray, still and moving at the same time. Clearly she had found the light in her soul and embraced all the different colors in her heart. Beautiful. See, we seniors have a lot to offer!

I smiled and nudged him, then petted Glider, who had come near. "What also struck me was that she responded quite intensely to the images projected on the screen in the theater, even before they appeared. Later I found research from the Heart-Math Institute in California—"

Ah yes, the heart already knows before the brain starts to process what the senses make us see, hear, feel, taste, and smell. Intelligence doesn't only reside in our skull, my friend. It's all over our body; the heart, the gut, in every single cell. Science has only scrapped the surface. There's so much more to discover. Please, continue your story.

"After Napels and Athens, Jerusalem was up next. Some five hundred people alighted from more than ten buses that had taken us from the harbor to the center of the holy city. She sat alone the whole trip over. When we arrived, I noticed no one was helping her off the bus, so I took her by the hand and stayed with her for the entire afternoon. This pattern repeated itself for most of our days together. I was saddened to see that so many who consider themselves to be 'spiritual seekers' didn't see the needs of the person sitting right beside them. Maybe

*The Indomitable Silence*

they felt sorry for her, I don't know, but how does that help? Isn't it true that compassion asks for hands that act on what the heart sees?"

Oh, very poetic! I like that. What happened next?

"On the third day in Israel, we went to the Jordan River, where the apostle John had baptized Jesus. She was one of the first in the water, although it took her much longer than others to change clothes. After her baptism, she started swimming and singing like a child. Ha! Her joy and playfulness were so captivating that many joined in spontaneously, and they all danced together in the river, all because of her! Finally people got a glimpse of her inner beauty, and, I hope, their own too."

This woman is triumph personified! Go on.

"A few days later the ship docked in Malta. We had been ashore all day, sightseeing on the island, and when we met each other at dinner late in the evening, I asked about her day. I'll never forget her answer. She had been dancing in her cabin the entire time, all by herself! The purser had put on her favorite music from the sixties, and then she had danced her heart out. It made me wonder about the times I had danced all by myself, just for the sheer fun of it. Her zest for life was like a mirror to me.

"She taught me, without lofty words, that we don't need any particular reason to be happy. She danced simply because she loved dancing. She smiled simply because she loved how it made her feel. Her joy came from the inside. There was no one to impress, no one to please, no one to convince. And yet it did all those things for me. She was totally at peace with herself and her life, although she was still hopeful to see the daylight again one day.

"This wonderful woman didn't consider her blindness a curse; instead she saw it as a blessing. She didn't ask why nor search for a deeper

*The Indomitable Silence*

meaning, but simply accepted the situation as it was. She had moved from resistance to acceptance, from struggle to peace, from pain to joy. She had traveled the shortest, yet sometimes longest, journey we all have to make one day."

She journeyed into her heart and heard its fierce whisper — the indomitable silence that nothing can ever take away — and she was strong enough to listen and surrender to it.

*The Indomitable Silence.* I sat quietly, letting those words settle on me like a dove resting on my shoulder. D put an arm around me and squeezed with protective camaraderie, then he winked and smacked me on the back.

Keep that one close to you.

"Thanks, I just may." D picked up Glider and ruffled his fur. The little fellah settled in contentedly. We quietly took in the scenery and the fresh low clouds that had descended on the valley, causing that dreamy dappling of sunlight across the lake and mountains. I loved being here. The vastness, the silence, the beauty. It all opened my heart.

There's more to the story, isn't there?

"That heart-bound journey had defining moments and turning points, like one night when I saw my girls join her at dinner. After a delightful meal together, they took her by the arm and guided her to her room. She hadn't asked for help. The girls just did it! I was filled with such pride, and I'm sure their hearts opened a little more that night. That's what any parent wants, to have life be as full as possible for their children. And to see them grow in love, compassion, and kindness.

"On another occasion she shared with me that the secret to her serenity was in the silence in her head. She no longer was enslaved by the insistent, raucous voices of worry, anger, and judgment. She

*The Indomitable Silence*

didn't care anymore what they said and the havoc they used to cause. She was done with those tyrants! And the less concerned she was about them, the more they left her alone, and the more free she felt. In that distance came the space to fall into her heart where she and love found each other.

"Now this wonderful woman was at peace and grateful for what life had given her, no longer resentful and angry at what it had taken away. And I was grateful she had come into my life. She showed me that although we often can't control or even make sense of life's challenges, we do control how to live in love and lightness, and then offer that as a gift to the world."

You can't put the totality of life into the house of logic. But you can open the heart into a cabin of love. Speaking of which, let's go back. More clouds are coming and I'm getting a bit chilled just sitting here. "Peace in motion," as she said!

The three of us got to our feet and made our way down the trail, huddling together to team up against the now buffeting wind. I was a little concerned about D, as he seemed very tired and depleted, his breathing becoming heavier by the minute. Strangely, our descent felt longer than the climb up. Puzzling over this gave way to thoughts about my own fortunes in life. Sure, I'd had my share of challenges and setbacks, but relatively speaking, I was in good shape. Though I knew gratitude should be my constant companion, I couldn't help but ask questions about success in conventional terms.

"Some spiritual teachers tell us a life of happiness, abundance, and success is our birthright. We deserve it! But I wonder, what about people who struggle with their health, their relationships, the loss of a loved one, or end up on the streets with despair and loneliness as their only friends? What about those who are born in circumstances with next to nothing? Not enough food, no clean water, no safety, no money, no freedom? Did they do something wrong to *deserve* that

*The Indomitable Silence*

kind of life? Or were they just born under the wrong stars and given a bad deal?" I looked at him, but except for a smile, he didn't answer. A bit miffed by this, I continued. "Do we really know why life unfolds the way it does? Kindness is returned with rudeness, generosity with dishonesty, loyalty with rejection. And on it goes..."

You seem to have forgotten what I just said, that you can't resolve life's mysteries with the instrument of logic. And it's not the grand life-purpose you need to discover or the major breakthrough you're waiting for. It's the simple, little things that can transform each single moment from something small to something big, something meaningless to something meaningful. Your German friend clearly understood that.

"She's happy every morning to have another day to live. As her clock is ticking, she realizes each and every moment, difficult or easy, provides her with an opportunity to find more acceptance, more peace, more joy. She's aware of her mortality and no longer afraid to die. You know what she shared with me about dying?"

She probably said she doesn't fear death, as she looks forward to being able to see again, and to do more heart-work on the other side. She has no regrets, no unfinished business, no untouched dreams. She's ready to go home at anytime.

"That's exactly what she told me! She said when she let go of the anger and resentment that were poisoning her mind, peace and happiness found her. She refused to burden her joy by holding on to the past. She let it all go overboard like a drop of vinegar in the vast ocean. I still remember that one sentence, as the words are engraved in my memory. She said freedom lies in acceptance, and grace arrives when the pathway to the heart is cleared. Isn't that beautiful?"

*The Indomitable Silence*

Glider, not at all impressed by these words of wisdom, barked at something in the air that apparently only he could see. D just smiled. "What's that all about?"

Once in a while he sees an angel or two. Nothing to be concerned about. The ladies are probably looking down at him, amused. They are protectors, too, so they like dogs, even though they startle him sometimes. I always get a kick out of this.

The cold wind was slowly getting to me, so I was happy to see the cabin coming into view in the fading afternoon light, noting to myself with relief the windows were closed. But before he could play out one of his space tricks and vanish, or have me transported somewhere, I asked him about something I still hadn't been able to control, or wipe out. "How have you handled fear in your life?"

Even after meeting Jesus, you are still afraid? Gosh!

"Hey, I'm back on Earth now, so give me a break!"

I'm just teasing you. You really want to know?

"Of course. Fear is probably the biggest obstacle to happiness, don't you think?"

It's a biggie, for sure, but it doesn't need to be that way. In my case, fear let go of me once the higher frequency of love flourished within me.

He turned quiet and kept walking. After a little while, I found myself disappointed and irked by his rather brief, vague explanation, and my impatience took over. "That's it?"

What else did you expect me to say?

*The Indomitable Silence*

"Well, there are so many ways in which people try to free themselves from fear. Countless courses, workshops, practices—"

Do they work?

I supposed from his curt question he was growing a little impatient with me, too. "How do you mean?"

Have all those "tricks and tips" actually worked for people? Because if not, I don't need to hear about them.

We had arrived at his cabin. D put his hand on the door and stopped, looking at me closely, his vibrant blue eyes narrowing with focus. He was clearly anticipating my next attempt to gain some more clarity. "Uh … I would have to ask them. But as far as I can see, it hasn't been that effective. The world is still full of fear."

Right on! You can't get rid of fear with the mind or body only. You can analyze it, cut it to pieces, know where it's coming from, scream, shout, and shiver, et cetera, et cetera, but all this won't set you free. Imagine entering a dark room and bumping repeatedly against the furniture. You may eventually figure out a safe route, after bruising your legs and stumbling around, but wouldn't it be better to just turn on the light? Come, let's go inside.

He opened the door latch with a loud *clack*, and in we went. Glider came with us this time. Happy to be included, he scampered around for a moment and then curled up in a far corner. D went to the stove area and, as usual, began preparing some coffee. I took my seat, trying to peer through the dim light inside.

I told you, you have to turn on the light. And take action, of course, or you'll end up standing in the cold doorway, wondering where the coffee and cakes are. Ha ha.

145

*The Indomitable Silence*

D stopped what he was doing and went to the chest at the foot of his bed. As he walked, his shadow danced in the glow of the oil lamp, and I realized how much I loved the warm atmosphere it brought to the room. Reaching into the chest, he took out a rope and tossed it on the floor, then returned to the kitchen.

Now you can see this is a rope. But if you stepped on it in the dark, you would probably jump and scream like a monkey, thinking it was a snake. You see where I'm going with this?

"I guess you're trying to show me that clarity and fear can't go together."

Fear is imagination going the wrong way.

"But what if someone jumps you with a knife?" D brought over a tray with the coffees and some small sugary cookies.

Well, if someone's trying to kill you, you must do your best to kick the shit out of them!

"Ha ha. Well yes, but—"

But metaphorically, you can't then assume everyone is going after you. Dance with the angels, but don't forget to dance with the dragons as well. See their faces, feel their moves, hear their growls. Be with them and bring them into the light, for what is brought into the light becomes the light. Don't judge, don't identify, don't resist, just be present and alert. The dragons are not in control of your cabin. All you need is the light of attention, the intention to move, and the courage to do so. You've been there before, that place of paralyzing darkness.

I swallowed hard at the memory D had so easily called to my mind. As he went back to the kitchen to get a spoon, I recalled the past challenges in my business; first the loss at the stratagem of a

*The Indomitable Silence*

finance fraudster, and then the attack by an unscrupulous competitor who took us to court for years of hard battle. Again I could feel my fist clench and my eyes go steely. D turned, approached the table, dropped the spoon, and pounded his fists on the table to brace himself. He stared fiercely at me as a comrade might before a battle.

*And what did you do?! I've seen it, but I want to hear it from you.*

My heart was pounding. I inhaled deeply and focused on my core, relaxed my fist, looked up at him, and exhaled. "I remembered why I was there, leading the company. My companion and I had started with next to nothing, except for a tremendous amount of passion and a few skills, and we had built it into something beautiful with highly satisfied customers all over the country. People worked hard for us, giving lots of their time and energy toward our success. My people counted on me. My family relied on me, so I had to master my emotions, manage the chaos, control the damage. But beneath this intense fear and rage there was… There was…"

*There was love! A thousand scoundrels are no match when the heart leads the charge. Now find that again.*

"I must have pushed a lot of these emotions deep inside and shut the door, because sometimes I still feel that pain. What to do?"

*The only way out is the way in.*

"The only…?"

Gruffly, D marched from wall to wall, thrusting each window wide open. He then sat down with a thud on the chair, evidence that his vigor had returned with alarming swiftness. I realized it was the sense of purpose and urgency that kept him going. I took a sip of coffee and chewed hard on a cookie. The warm green light filled our space over the table, and we were transported…

*The Indomitable Silence*

I found myself in an office I had never been in before, but somehow it felt like my own. Books lined the walls, much like my library at home. D was with me, sitting in a chair in the corner as I scanned the shelves and took in the titles: Krishnamurti, Rumi, the Bible, but also some contemporary jewels from Eckhart Tolle and Wayne Dyer. I noticed one section where a stack of books was hidden behind a tiny door with a label *Footprints From Heaven* in front of it. I turned to face D as he began speaking.

All these books bring you back to the essence of who you are. This is how the world is healed: by touching hearts one person at a time, helping to change the world in them. It reminds me of a story of Mahatma Gandhi...

He paused to gather himself, taking on an aura of reverence for the man who clearly had meant so much to India, and whose legacy continues to inspire many in the world today, including me.

One day a Hindu man came to Gandhi, who had been on hunger-strike for two weeks because of the recent killings between Muslims and Hindus. The man's heart was broken and his eyes were spitting fire. A Muslim warrior had killed his only son, and his heart was burning with desire for revenge. Gandhi listened to the man's fiery words, and then invited him to sit on his bed. He put his hand upon the man's heart and told him with a soft, frail voice:

"Hate and killing won't bring your son back. Go to the orphanage, find a young boy to take care of, and love him as your own son." Gandhi paused for a moment, as if to give the man some time to make space for the words that still make me cry. He said, "But make sure it's a Muslim boy."

The man broke down in tears and fell into the arms of the great soul. Gandhi was so wise that he knew the man's intense grief and hate could only be overcome by an even greater act of compassion

*The Indomitable Silence*

and care. Only the same love he had for his lost child could heal his broken heart.

Moved by D's story, I remembered a family trip to India, where we visited Gandhi's office in Mumbai. On its walls were many pictures and countless testimonials of people who'd had the privilege of walking in the little man's footsteps, proof that anyone can achieve the seemingly impossible when the heart is driven by a mission far greater than the mind can ever conceive. A heart that never breaks, no matter how often it bends. And a body that never gives in, no matter how often it is defeated. Slowly, tentatively, I sat in the chair behind the desk, folded my hands in front of me, and continued to listen to my old, wise friend.

People like Mahatma Gandhi, Nelson Mandela, the Dalai Lama, all give us hope because despite the enormous suffering and sacrifices they have to make, they remain strong, balanced, and peaceful amid a hostile and oftentimes violent environment.

"It's amazing these men can see the light shining through even the darkest clouds, and remain kind and forgiving toward those who commit such heinous crimes against humanity, even their own families; that their suffering hasn't turned them bitter, and hungry for revenge."

These great souls are able to go beyond their own pain and tap into a force which is beyond fear and reason. But we can do the same! It just requires a heart and mind that will not rest until we rise into our highest potential. That's how the world will heal. One heart, one mind, at a time.

"I'm not sure we have the right leaders in place to do what you just said."

*The Indomitable Silence*

No! It's not the politicians or peace demonstrators who will end conflict and bring peace. It's not the economic experts or bankers who will heal the economy and bring abundance. It's not the doctors or psychiatrists who will cure our diseases and bring health. And it's not the priests or spiritual teachers who will save our souls and bring happiness. It is us, my friend — you and me! The power is in our hands, in each and every mind and heart. Because we are one. We are the One! We are—

*"Goede morgen, Angelo. Hoe gaat het met je?"*

Taken by surprise, I shot a look at the door and quickly stood up. It was a man I recognized from my old home town, Maastricht. I was going to answer in English, *I'm fine, thank you*, but quickly flipped to my native tongue.

*"Goede morgen. Prima, dank je wel. En hoe gaat het met u?"*

*"Heel goed, dank je wel,"* the man responded, smiling pleasantly, before carrying on down the hall of what looked like a center of some kind. I stood blinking, my mouth open.

Remember how you wondered about the people whose lives you touched? You need not worry. They saw what you did for them, how much you cared. Your old staff showed you their gratitude when they threw you a welcome back birthday party... Wait, has that happened yet?

Just then, a woman poked her head into the office, but she spoke English as we had an exchange similar to the one I'd had with the friendly gentleman: "Good morning, Angelo! How are you today?"

"Good morning, uh…" I stumbled on her name but recognized her face from a recent storytelling evening in Kelowna, where she was

150

*The Indomitable Silence*

one of the speakers. Pushing past my confusion with good manners, I continued. "I'm doing well, thank you. How are you?"

"Doing just great, thanks. Looks like a nice day out there, hey? See ya!" She bopped away, clearly in a good mood as well.

Dumbfounded, I reached into my pocket and pulled out my iPhone. The date was Nov 12, 2018! "What—? How—? And where—?"

Yes.

"*Yes*? That's all you've got?"

Well, Chiara will be away at university, of course. But here—

"Is where?"

That remains to be seen. These visions are not absolutes but reflections of what lingers around in your heart, and the choice between Canada and the Netherlands is that reality right now. The outcome is as yet unknown. So is the specific nature of your future work. Your path is to connect and help create well-being in people, in communities. To hear the words "good morning" in the universal language of the heart!

Smiling at my raised eyebrows, D got up and took two books down from the shelves — *Journey into the Soul* and *The Indomitable Silence* — and handed them to me. I held them in my hands and looked at the hypnotic blue of the first one and the soft, warm green cover of the second. My name was printed on both.

Your first and your second! There's a third, but let's not get ahead of ourselves. I see you're still absorbing it all. This is the reason for everything, my friend. You write to touch people. Wherever you live, you're breathing these books. Look...

*The Indomitable Silence*

D grabbed *The Indomitable Silence* from my hand and opened it on a particular page. I felt dizzy, as though I were whirling in a time loop. Gathering myself, I sat down and read:

*We arrived at our destination in the early morning. I parked the car and we walked through the big entrance of a picturesque medieval castle. It was a cold and foggy winter day. A couple of days earlier I had surprised my parents by flying in to Amsterdam. I called them when I arrived at the airport. Mum answered the phone, speechless. Three hours later they picked me up at the train station in their hometown. Usually I would visit them once a year, but this time it had been only four months since my last trip here. This break from our usual pattern filled us all with a palpable feeling of magic and possibility.*

*Now, as in the good old days, my father and I were on our way to our first ever silent retreat. The immense park welcomed us, and we appeared to be the only visitors. I chuckled to myself. Of course we were the first to arrive. My father would never stand for tardiness, ours most of all. We started the day with coffee and cookies, and waited as more people arrived. After a few greetings, the day of silence started at 10 a.m. and we were not to talk until 8 p.m. After about an hour, my thoughts had slowed down and I felt the urge to start writing. I took a pad of paper and a pen, and waited for words to come. The floodgates flew open and I wrote in a flurry of joy. Soon I noticed a strange change in the composition of the room, as my peripheral vision seemed to work like a personal guard to my focused effort.*

*But I kept writing, paying no more attention to what was going on around me. When I was done, I looked down at the words and realized this was the passage I had been working on since I had met D. Rolling the pen between my thumb and index finger, I sat up, leaned back, and looked around at the familiar coziness of my friend's place. D said nothing from the corner, where he now sat drinking a coffee. We smiled at each other as I pushed the pad to the middle of the wooden table and imagined the words flying into the air and out through the window:*

*The Indomitable Silence*

*I am the silence.*
*No matter the wars in your head.*
*No matter the clouds in your heart.*
*No matter the storms in your life.*
*I am beyond all that.*

*I am the silence.*
*I am beyond concern, but I care for you.*
*I am beyond desire, but I long for your heart.*
*I am beyond thought, but I dance through your mind.*
*I am beyond language, but I breathe life into your words.*

*I am the silence.*
*I am the joy in your smile.*
*I am the sadness in your tears.*
*I am the whisper in your stillness.*
*I am the love in your courage.*

*I am the silence.*
*I am beyond form, but all life arises from me.*
*I am beyond space, but every heart finds a home in me.*
*I am beyond time, but all there is begins and ends with me.*
*I am beyond light, but every soul finds its way through me.*

*I am the silence.*
*I lose myself, so you can find me.*
*I forget myself, so you can come to know me.*
*I divide myself, so you can be with me everywhere.*
*I darken myself, so you can see my light in everything.*

*The Indomitable Silence*

*I am the silence.*
*I am your vision, and you are my eyes.*
*I am your heart, and you are my hands.*
*I am your mirror, and you are my image.*
*I am your conscience, and you are my voice.*

*I am the Source.*
*I am the Self.*
*I am.*

"I am," I heard myself say, as I looked up from the desk in front of me, pushed the pad to the middle of the wooden table, and, to my delighted surprise, realized I was in D's cabin, just as I had written! It was as though the words formed deep within had manifested in reality, and not for the first time I witnessed the heart's ability to create pure magic through our hands. Looking across the cabin, I was happy to see my friend sitting in the corner, drinking coffee, Glider at his feet. We smiled at each other.

You forgot to mention Glider in that section, but everything else was pretty good.

Our little canine companion looked up, woofed, and kept his eyes on me while I tore the top sheet off and folded it into my coat pocket. As I stood up to go, D straightened in his chair and set his coffee down on the kitchen counter. Then he rose, and I could tell he wanted to share his own inspired words. I waited by the door. Eerily, he seemed to look right through me as he channeled words from beyond.

I am the one who looks through your eyes and breathes through your lungs. I am the one who dwells in a heavenly state while part of me is also on Earth, with you. I am the one who dances in the light and shadow, forever untouched. We share the same soul. We are one! We are...

*The Indomitable Silence*

There was a firm and crisp knock at the cabin door. I looked over my shoulder, then back at D, who grinned and nodded for me to answer it. I turned, slowly placed my hand on the door handle, heard the loud *clack*, and pulled...

# OUT OF MY HEAD

The sound of knocking still fresh in my ears, I opened the door and there he was, standing with a big smile on his face and car keys in his hand. What? Where was I? Looking around, I realized I was no longer in the cabin; I was in my own home but still wearing my outdoor clothes. Hearing a dog bark, I looked over my shoulder, half expecting to see Glider scratching and hopping on the wooden floor. But it was my own pooch, Cinnamon, now up on his feet in the front hall. I shushed him and told him to stay. Turning around I looked quizzically at D. At least he was using the door this time. I peered past him and was now shocked to see a red Lamborghini in our driveway!

Full of surprises, hey? I used to be well connected. Still have a few friends—

"In high places, I see."

Well, mostly in low places. My buddy Ray has a few of these beauties, and once in a while he lets me drive this red beast. Love it!

"Ray?! You mean the guy with the ponytail and tattoos all over his arms?"

Yeah, that's him. Older fellah.

*Out of My Head*

"I guess, hard to tell his age. Met him at a poker game in pastor Mike's house. Interesting guy for sure! He's been in some very low places and felt more than the human heart should have to bear. The next day he showed up here with a yellow Lamborghini, and immediately I called Chiara. She loves fancy cars. Never seen her coming down the stairs so quickly. Ha! Didn't even put her shoes on. Jumped in right away, smiling ear to ear as they sped off. Wow … what a synchronicity of events!"

Indeed! I always thought luxury cars were a waste of money, but hey, why not seize some childlike fun when you get the chance? I don't own it; it doesn't own me. We're just passing through, my friend. So let's go!

Sensing Fanny and the girls were out, I checked for my keys and closed the door behind me. D opened the car doors using the remote control, we slid into the white leather seats, and within seconds the engine fired up with such power you would think we were on a tarmac. In a flash we were passing through the front gate, out into the neighborhood. I could see the wind blowing in the trees up on the mountain, but strangely I didn't feel the wind or cold, even though the sunroof was open. It was as if part of me was sitting in the car and the other part wasn't.

I had heard of people having lucid dreams, and I wondered whether this was something I was experiencing. After a fifteen-minute drive around the mountainside neighborhood, we were back in the driveway, then making our way toward the front door. D wrapped an arm around my shoulder.

What did you think of that?

"That was a thrill. Thank you!" Despite the exuberance of the ride still in him, I could feel his growing fragility; life was slowly starting to make its way out. I swallowed the lump of worry in my throat and

*The Indomitable Silence*

tried not to think about it. He sensed my concern and changed the topic, for my sake.

The doorway torches are wonderful with their classical look. Quite special. I'm sure you didn't get those at Walmart.

"No, handmade by a blacksmith living farther north in the valley."

You can see the care and craftsmanship. Only someone with a great heart for what he's doing can make such a piece of art.

I recalled the workshops and studios in D's heavenly dream, and I understood what he meant. "When we bought this place, we tracked down the artist and paid him a visit at his cabin workshop near Vernon. Single guy; just him and his dog, living in the woods. In fact, he looked a lot like you, except that he had a beard. And he wasn't that old."

Thanks, buddy! Appreciate your words. Feeling a lot younger now.

"I'm glad you do." We both laughed, walked in, and took off our shoes as Cinnamon came running. What happened next was remarkable. Usually he jumps all over people when they enter, eagerly anticipating some playtime, but not this time. Instead, he stopped and sat still, waiting patiently as D never took his gaze off him. My friend held his hand out like an eagle's trainer. Cinnamon came obediently and bowed his head to let D scratch his ears.

Good boy. Good boy.

"Come…" We made our way out into the capacious living room overlooking the lake, the mountains, and the city. D removed his coat and motioned his head toward the sofa. I nodded it was fine. He laid it down and looked at the high windows and glass doors leading to the back patio. Saying nothing, he beheld the panoramic vista, smiled,

*Out of My Head*

almost with recognition on his face, and then walked over with his hands clasped courteously behind his back.

You should be very grateful to live in a place like this. Absolutely stunning. What a view!

A memory flashed across my mind, and I saw myself driving my first car at the age of thirty. It was a thirteen-year-old Nissan, nothing fancy, but to me it was a brand new Mercedes. I had just started the business and needed a car to take me to customers throughout the country. I didn't care how old it was or how ugly it looked; it was a precious work of art for me, serving me when I needed it. Those were good times. Reflecting now on my good fortune, in a home I wouldn't have dreamed of as a young boy, I mused about my ongoing search for happiness. D turned to face me.

I know your heart doesn't feel quite at home. Hey, you answered a note in a mailbox, after all. Clearly you're still searching.

Again, D had read me well. I nodded. "I'll show you around." We took a short tour around the house, making casual comments about various architectural and decorative features here and there. Cinnamon followed along curiously. Then, as we returned to the entrance hall, D pointed to a room to the side, away from the main living space. "Ah yes, I'll show you where I do feel perfectly at home, though I believe you *have* seen it briefly." I grinned at him and opened the door. As we entered, with one single push of a button the lights dimmed and the symphonic music of Anathema filled the space. Cinnamon barked. "Shh, stay Cinnamon. Good boy." I closed the door behind us.

Wow, what a place! And yes, I do remember it. Nice to be invited this time, though.

*The Indomitable Silence*

D winked at me and began wandering around, scanning the whole space with an almost reverential demeanor: the six leather chairs in front of the curved projector screen, the granite bar-top, the well-crafted cupboards, the hand-painted ceiling, the four torches made by the same artist as the ones outside. The expression on his face showed how deeply moved he was by the beauty and the sense of sequestered purpose. His gaze then fell squarely upon the glass bookcase at the far end.

"It's all I've got. Not a big reader, I prefer to live the words." We exchanged a knowing grin as he approached the shelves and scanned the book spines with curiosity.

Interesting! These are the evidence of your quest. One day yours will be here, too.

"I hope so. Trying my best. Come, have a seat." We settled into two reclining plush chairs and let the music wash over us. I closed my eyes and wondered when I was going to wake from this dream. The thought passed as quickly as it had formed, though, but I didn't care. Consciousness is fluid, I remembered, and being in the moment was all that mattered to me now. Clearly something mattered to D, too, as I soon heard my friend crying softly. I looked over at him.

I feel—

The lump in his throat made it impossible for him to finish the sentence. "You feel what?"

I feel ... them.

"Who?"

My children. I...

*Out of My Head*

Not only his voice was shaking by now, but his whole body was overwhelmed by emotion. Tears came running down his cheeks. "Oh my—"

I can feel them, my ... little angels. They are here.

The tough, adventurous Lamborghini guy had turned into a trembling, grieving father, and all I could do was just be with him, hold the space, and say nothing. For a long time silence nestled in between us. I know his heart was aching, but at the same time, it was so beautiful, so serene. Together, wordless, yet so connected. I could almost hear the growing whisper in my heart, and his, until his heart couldn't stay quiet anymore.

It's this space. There's something magical about it. The energy is so powerful.

"It's where I do all my writing."

I know. So much love. That's what connected me with my children.

"They left?" I felt sad for him that the contact might already have been broken.

Yes. They probably have some other stuff to do. It's happened before. It's okay.

His words brought me back to the experience of one of my travels with Atmos where I met my grandma on the other side. I knew how special it was for both of us, and I had a pretty good sense of what was going on inside of him right now. "You know why they were here?"

It feels like they wanted to bring their energy to this space. Something to do with your books. Not sure.

*The Indomitable Silence*

He closed his eyes and bowed his head, as if he needed silence to detect and decipher the words beyond human hearing. After what felt like at least a minute, I heard a deep sigh, and he mumbled something. It was very soft, and I couldn't make out what he was saying. Nor did I have any idea whom he was communicating with. But it wasn't me. Another stretch of silence passed before he directed his words toward me again.

They want you to know they'll help you. With your book. It needs their playful, light-hearted energy to balance out the somewhat heavier parts. It's like a symphony or a painting. All the sounds and colors need to be in harmony. I'm so grateful they came. And not only for me.

As he spoke these last words, the atmosphere in the room became even stronger, and I saw how the warm green light connected our hearts. But there was more. The light also came from above, but I couldn't see a source. Maybe... I dropped my train of thought, closed my eyes, and took in the beauty of the moment. Then a quirky question whispered in my mind. I quietly laughed, not wanting to hurt his feelings, but the words were already there. "Wait, why isn't your wife ever with you?" Unexpectedly, D's mood turned mirthful. He looked relieved.

Not sure. She was hard enough to keep up with in life. Ha ha! Maybe she's throwing a party on the other side. She loves food ... and laughs.

I was glad the ambiance had cleared up and his cheeky playfulness had returned. "Sounds like Fanny!" We looked at each other and laughed heartily. "If she comes home now, things will get interesting." We sat without speaking for a while, until my thoughts brought me back to the ripples in my heart. "She likes it here, and my kids are split in their preferences. For now! Kids change their minds overnight. It's complicated. Where is home?"

*Out of My Head*

Home is here. It's where the heart blossoms.

"Whose heart? Hers, theirs, mine?"

You can't say where one heart ends and the others begin. In true love, there's one heart everyone shares. And that's the one which tells you where home is.

Once more I was surprised he was able to organize his thoughts so quickly and clearly, and focus again on my path. I pondered the idea of a shared heart and what I had experienced with D in the other realm. The unshakable love between a little boy, on the verge of dying, and his father. The unspeakable sadness of a family's heart, ripped apart by the suicide of their child, the regrets, the guilt, and ultimately the healing. And of course, being with my own little angels in the City of Lights. How they ran over to me and we had such fun together, playing, teasing, but always loving. I let the images and emotions pass by and focused on my heart. Clarity and calmness came over me, and I knew no matter what the future held for us, we would all be okay. We had love and that would guide us home, wherever that might be.

Just then the screen came on! Looking for the remote control, I realized D had done this himself. He smiled and pointed at a scene now coming into view. It was Alyssa with me on a river ferry back in the Netherlands. She looked a few years older and I realized I was seeing the future, and yet I was feeling the emotions now through the screen...

*We had already finished breakfast and were riding our bikes, feeling lucky to have caught a warm, sunny day with a faint breeze. After ten minutes, we reached the river and boarded the ferry to take us across. Once we had left the quay, two older women came from behind a vehicle, wheeling their bikes happily in our direction. They appeared to be sisters who had decided to spend the day riding*

*The Indomitable Silence*

*together. After a few pleasantries about the weather, one of them asked where we lived, and I told her we were visiting from Canada where we had lived for the past five fears. She asked how it was to be back home, and I said I didn't know where my home really was.*

*Sometimes for the heart to recognize the truth it already knows, we need to hear from someone else, preferably a stranger. This was one of those moments. The words she used were not original, but she spoke them with such unflinching certainty in her eyes that their clarity seemed to run right through me: "Home is where the heart is." So, where was my heart? I knew it was here, in this little village, in our old house, but it was also with my family.*

*She explained further that her son used to live in a big house with more luxury than he could ever have imagined, but his heart was not there. He felt empty inside, and after some time he decided to leave. Now he lived in a much smaller home, but his heart was full again. Her story touched a tender string, and I knew this was not a mere coincidence. I needed to hear this. As the ferry touched the opposite riverbank, I thanked her for her kind words, and we all said goodbye. As she and her sister disembarked, she turned back and said, "Don't forget to follow your heart, wherever it leads you." Then Alyssa and I were on our way again.*

*We rode through the green landscape until we reached a quiet spot where a few boats were anchored in a little harbor. We stopped, got off our bikes, and lay down on the grass. A man was fishing while his wife was enjoying the sunshine in a lazy chair next to him. A few cows and sheep were grazing in the green meadows, and a boat was passing by on the river. We held hands as a light breeze caressed our faces and tickled the wildflowers around us. Basking in the gentle glow of the sunshine, no words were spoken, but our hearts were speaking. After a while, she laid her head down on my shoulder. She was so beautifully close, and my heart took a picture.*

*Out of My Head*

My head was spinning. I turned toward D, trying to compose myself. "When does that happen? Two years from now? Three?"

*The heart is beyond time, so don't ask yourself if or when this will happen. Look at the pictures in your heart and listen to what they have to say. Bring your light into the family's heart, and don't dismiss a future in Canada just yet. I know you've struggled, because you have a strong will, but if you would surrender...*

"Then perhaps doors I didn't even know existed will open up?"

*Right on! See with your heart, plan with your head, and build with your hands.*

"And drink with your mouth! Let's have some coffee."

*Ha! Well done. No need to figure it all out today. Yes, a coffee sounds lovely.*

"The least I can do after all the cups of java in your place." D grinned graciously as we got up and went out to the living room. There he picked up my guitar, which hadn't been played in fifteen years. Cinnamon followed, sitting near D as he sat down and started to strum, his face calm and peaceful. While the coffee brewed, I looked at him from the kitchen, closed my eyes, and felt myself slipping into reverie. The soft sounds filled the background as past images appeared before my mind's eye. Images of me sitting on a park bench in Maastricht, where I lived in my late twenties.

It was a time in my life when I felt so peaceful, so in touch with myself, that I sometimes long to go back to those days. I could sit there for hours, watching passersby and listening to the sounds of the city. Life was simple, with no distracting thoughts nor full daily schedules and responsibilities. Suddenly these memories dissolved into those of the city park in Kelowna, where I also had my moments

*The Indomitable Silence*

of serenity. Where I had met... D continued strumming and began picking as he spoke.

Live in the moment, brother. Fond memories are fine, but you must move forward through what's in front of you now.

"Oh, those thoughts and memories. They can be a handful! I wish I had more control over them. I would definitely kick a few ones out, I can tell you that!" For a moment or two, D seemed to be processing what I had just said. He then looked at me inquisitively, raised his eyebrows, and smiled mischievously.

Have you ever wondered what it would be like to be a thought?

I grimaced at him and began preparing the coffees. "Come again?"

Have you ever given it any consideration to how a thought would feel and behave if it were a person?

"Of course not. What a silly question!"

Why is it silly?

His facial expression suddenly changed, making it quite clear he was dead serious, which made me dig in even harder. "Come on! A thought is not a person, just something that arises in the brain."

Something that can bother you a lot, obviously.

"Yes. So?"

Well, you haven't managed to free yourself from your thoughts so far, have you? We've spoken a lot about the heart, but to get there—

*Out of My Head*

"Nobody is without thoughts!" I felt myself getting a bit annoyed, and even his little guitar ditty, which sounded pleasant in the beginning, was starting to get to me.

I didn't mean being free of thoughts, but the ability to free yourself from them.

"Neither!" Maybe it was because of my blunt response, but D stopped playing, set down the guitar, and looked at me intently, a hint of playfulness returning to his face.

How would you feel if you knew how to do that?

"That would be wonderful," I answered, with a noticeable bite of sarcasm. The coffees ready, I walked into the living room and placed them on the glass table between us. "Enjoy your coffee, by all means."

Thanks, but I'm serious.

"I've noticed. So what do you suggest?" I rushed a few sips, anticipating something rather unexpected and bizarre was about to happen.

You and I are going to have a conversation with the voice in your head. It's gonna be fun!

"Fun … right."

Just give it a try! What have you got to lose?

It was obvious I wasn't gonna win this battle, so I gave in. "Okay, what do you want me to do?"

Yes! Finally! Well, I'll be the thought, and you … just be you. All right?

*The Indomitable Silence*

"Sure, why not."

Which thought would you like to explore?

"You pick, no guitar pun intended." D shot me a withering look, and took a quick sip of coffee.

Let's do a fearful thought. That's always a tough one. Come on, ask me something.

"I feel foolish."

Ah, just go with it. And be yourself, attitude and all. I know you!

"Fine. Okay, where do you come from, Mr. Thought?"

I arise from the field of consciousness, where all thoughts are born and eventually die.

"Sounds like a fun place … to be *from*. So, you don't belong to me?"

I come and go; I belong to no one.

"Oh, come on! Of course you're mine! I know what I'm thinking."

Oh really? Do you know who comes after me?

"Uh … no. Why do you ask?"

Well, if you were in control, if I were a hundred percent your creation, you would know where I'm going and who comes after me, right? But you don't. And you know why? Because I arise spontaneously. I float through the mind with or without your permission. And there's nothing you can do about it, except…

"Except what?"

*Out of My Head*

When you change the atmosphere inside. I only enter where I feel comfortable, obeying the law of attraction. I'm a thought of fear, so I feel at home when there's fear hanging in the air.

"But I don't want you in *my home*." I blinked a couple of times as a cocoon of red light shrouded D, giving him a menacing look that filled me with dread and apprehension. I struggled to breathe.

I can see that. You argue, you resist, you fight. You even try to finish me off!

"I want you to leave me alone! You make me feel anxious and tense."

Why can't you just accept me for who I am? I have feelings, too, you know.

"I don't care about your feelings!"

I've noticed that as well. You first tried to chase me out of your head, and when I touched your heart, you even tried to drive me out of there. But I'm immune to willpower and resistance. They only make me stronger! And I call my buddies to back me up, if needed.

"You do what?" D's expression took on an oddly malicious aspect. My core tightened as he continued.

Hey, I have the right to live! So if you give me a hard time, I call my friends to give me a helping hand. See what happens when you attack one thought like me? You end up having to contend with an entire army! My gentle scream in your head becomes a massive war cry that takes over your entire system. How do you like me now?

"You're getting stronger. I want you out!"

You could use my energy, you know.

*The Indomitable Silence*

"I don't *want* to use you. You're awful."

If you could see me for who I am, you might actually appreciate what I can do for you. Maybe alert you to a potential danger, or activate your courage to overcome a big hurdle. I have many good reasons to be here. If only—

"You just want to hurt me like all of you do. You're making a mess in my head, and in my stomach."

Listen, my friend, I don't want to hurt you; I only want to be heard. And I'll stay until you get that!

"You are *not* my friend, *buddy.*"

I know you don't like me, but your resistance only pushes me deeper inside. Stop treating me like a piece of trash. I want to be free, just like you want to be free from me, but what can I do if you lock me up? I'll have to create havoc in your inner world, so I can get out. And I'm sorry, but at that point things are no longer within my control.

"Oh, so now it's *my* fault?!"

Please listen to what I have to say. Feel me, embrace me, or at least accept me if you can't love me. Give me some space, will you?

"That's the last thing I want, to give you even *more* space to grow."

No, creating space doesn't make me grow. It allows me to pass through the heart, and leave your home. Lean back and relax. I won't hurt you. Nothing can, really.

I leaned back in my chair and breathed deeply, looking across the coffee table. "Okay, you say you want to be accepted and heard. So

*Out of My Head*

what is it exactly you want me to hear?" The red around D began to soften slightly, as did his facial expression.

I don't understand. First you invited me in, you were in the right mood. But once I arrived, you started your crusade against me. It's very confusing and upsetting, to be honest.

When he spoke those last words, I started to feel a bit sorry for the young fellow. I saw where he was coming from, understood his struggles. He sounded almost human. And it hit me how lonely he must feel, being chased away most of his life by almost everyone. "I hear you, and I'll make sure my doors are open next time you visit me. I'll give you enough space to breathe, and you can stay as long as you want. I realize the universe is your home and my heart is but one of its rooms. I'll try to be a good host, but please don't be too hard on me, for I'm not at my best when you're around." D's face now showed surrender and gratitude. I waited for approval. "Do you feel you've been heard now?"

Yes. Thank you. I'm going to rest here a bit and then I'll be on my way.

"Where are you going?" D leaned back and shrugged.

I don't know, it's always a surprise who invites me in next. I'm like a bird, free to fly anywhere I want, until someone catches me in their mind and locks me up. I get defensive and the drama starts all over again.

"Hopefully I won't make that mistake again."

Oh, no. I think you've learned your lesson. We can be friends, you and me. Goodbye for now. I'll be back! And I won't be that tough on you anymore. I promise.

*The Indomitable Silence*

I noticed a big change in myself as I took in his now jovial expression. The tension in my chest had subsided and the harsh red glow around D had turned to warm green and violet. I hadn't intended to change the atmosphere; it had just happened! Somehow, from deep within, I had found acceptance and peace. Nor was I concerned about my girls walking in. I would simply introduce him as a friend of mine and Ray's. Besides, the car in the driveway would win Chiara over! D grinned, and I could see he had transitioned back to his usual self, at least as I knew him.

I think you just aced this ad hoc coaching exercise! Feel better?

"Ha! Yes, thank you." The two of us stayed in our reclined positions. Nothing was said for several moments, until I leaned forward and whispered, "*I am the silence.*" I winked at him. He winked back.

The sound of surrender. You've created space for peace and love to shine from within. Now you just need to find ways to let the light out and help others do the same. And start with those who are closest to you. You know who I mean.

"More coffee?"

No, more driving — let's go!

D smacked his hands on his legs and stood up with a sudden swiftness. Cinnamon jumped up and barked. "Shh, Cinnamon. It's okay." D crouched and patted his head.

Good boy. You remind me of my Glider, so sweet and supportive. Yes, I love you, too.

"Sit, Cinnamon." He looked at both of us, settled back down on the area rug, and stayed there as D and I grabbed our coats and went out. As I closed the door behind me, I was surprised to see it was now the

*Out of My Head*

handle of the car door I was holding. We were already in the car! I looked at D. The engine was rumbling with power.

I'm eager to get on the road, so I eliminated the driveway walk from this experience. Fun, hey? Being a liaison does have its privileges.

He smiled, put the car in gear, and we shot out of the driveway. *Woosh!* And we were off, speeding through the neighborhood toward the main mountain road. The jolt of velocity had awoken my concerned and questioning side, however. "Careful! There could be other cars, or kids."

Don't worry, we will see them.

Not completely convinced, I fell into vigilant silence, scanning the roadsides as we descended through the slopes and trees. Glancing over at D, I could see his hands and gaze were surprisingly steady. Noticing my scrutinizing stare, he smiled musingly.

People try to hide from their thoughts and emotions in all kinds of ways. They lose themselves in the noise of distractions, of work, of substances. They get drunk, over-eat, or plan to visit a Himalayan cave, which are all taken, by the way. Or, you can just hit the throttle and find inner peace amid the busy traffic of life. You are part of the modern world; it can't be avoided. So...

"We'd better enjoy the ride, as stressful as it can be at times."

Stress? Who's talking about stress?

"Uh ... I just mentioned it."

I don't want stress. So, I don't create it.

"Create it? Stress is not something you create, my dear friend, it's something that happens! There are stressful situations *out there,* you

*The Indomitable Silence*

know. It's not all peace and love in this world." D hit the accelerator and we careened down the mountain. "Hey, go easy!"

A man doesn't have a job. One problem, money. Therefore stress. Then, lucky him, he finds a job. Now, many problems, more stress. Another man is single. One problem, loneliness. Then, lucky him, a woman walks into his life and they get married. Now, ooooh...

He winked at me with a knowing smile. We both burst out in laughter. I loved how he could say so little but tell so much. And he wasn't done yet.

Listen. Stress is created from within, by the mind, and as soon as it hijacks your system, you try to manage it. It's called stress management, I believe. Ha! So tell me, why in the world would you manage something you don't even want? Finances, projects, time-schedules — all those things have value and need to be dealt with in a proper way. But stress? Come on! What's so valuable about stress? Oh my gosh!

"Don't ridicule this! You know darned well modern life isn't that easy." D stayed quiet and eased off the gas a little. I took his tacit cue that words were not helping right now, and settled into the ride. We came to the end of the main mountain road and turned onto the highway leading southwest out of the city. And though it appeared to be about mid-afternoon, the traffic was blissfully, albeit strangely, light. The sky was a magical mixture of sun and cloud, like my mind.

Imagine driving a car without a steering wheel and brakes. You're not in control of the vehicle, and can only hope the oncoming traffic will maneuver well and not hit you. Now that is a stressful situation!

"Uh, that's—"

*Out of My Head*

I'm only speaking figuratively here. When you are in control of your system, and I'm talking about the most sophisticated computer ever, the human mind and body, nothing outside needs to cause any stress. When someone crosses the street or the traffic light turns red, you stop. When there's a slow car in front of you, you pass it. When you've had enough, you get out. No big deal!

It just so happened D decided to overtake a slow pickup at this point. He picked up speed and didn't slow down when he returned to his own lane, smiling ear to ear. Although I wanted him to ease the pace, I also didn't want to lose our train of thought, so I threw out a line I had heard somewhere: "It's about context, not content."

Good point! Would be nicer if it were your own words, though.

He had read my mind again. "Well, you have anything to say about my *good point*?"

The content of any given situation is not always in your hands, but the context you give it, the way you process it internally and the energy you hold, is entirely your call. When you're peaceful, you bring peace to the table. And when you're fearful, you're likely to manufacture the very thing that stresses you out. I don't know about you, but I prefer to manifest what I wish to see, not what I don't want. Like a psychic potluck!

"Fanny would love that line."

Ha ha! Yes, my wife liked entertaining and food, too. Now, THAT is real!

"What's also real is that I prefer you to slow down, so we don't end up in the lake!" He remained annoyingly unfazed and unmoved.

No worries. I know this beauty from the inside out! That's why I can handle her, no matter the speed. And I like it fast! Just

*The Indomitable Silence*

as in real life. Intense, full throttle, emergency brake off! Alive and kicking, baby — like that eighties song by Simple Minds! Remember that one?

"Great band, love the song! It's cool we share the same taste in music, but right now my main concern is that we *stay* alive and kicking — and not so much on the accelerator!"

Who's the old man here? If I can't even chill out to thrill out in this magical car, they might as well put me in the ground now! Relax, I know what I'm doing.

"Okay, but you do know it has rained quite a bit, right? The road may be slippery."

Oh, you're thinking what could go wrong again. I'm just having a good time and enjoying all the beauty around me. Hey, you live in the Okanagan Valley! You should know what the sun can do in no time when the rain ends. Poof — dry and drivable beauty.

"Yes, it's breathtaking when that happens, I know. The rays burst around the broken clouds, creating ethereal edges. It's quite the view."

When you are that glowing hope on the edge of the clouds, when you have that unwavering sense of purpose, there's no stopping you. Be yourself and dare to show who you are! Dance, write, meditate, laugh, and cry. Walk in nature, go for a crazy ride, listen to music, take a shower—

"Well, I do that anyway. You know, to be fresh and presentable to—"

Agh, are you seriously nitpicking my wisdom?

"I'm just saying—"

*Out of My Head*

And I'm saying do anything that opens the heart! And do it with all the passion you've got! When you cry, then cry your heart out. When you smile, then smile so big that people wonder if you've lost it. And when you love, well, then ... I don't need to tell you what that looks like. Hey, there's even beauty in anger. I've seen you. It doesn't happen that often. But I love it! It's quite funny, actually. Ha ha.

"Are you kidding me?"

Nope! I enjoy everything done with the highest pitch of intensity. Look, here I am near the end of my life and I'm driving this baby like a thoroughbred in an open field.

"Uh, please stay on the *racetrack*."

Ha! I'm not being literal. And I'm not wasting any more precious time, my friend. Leaving it all out here on the road. And that's how you should live!

"Fine! Now could you please slow down a bit? I'm not quite at *your* level of intensity."

Gosh, you're nothing like your daughter. She loves speed! I bet she would have taken the wheel if I had let her.

"I'm glad you didn't."

Chill out! Get out of your head! That's the whole point of this ride. Don't you get it? Out of the head, and...

"Into the heart. I know."

Oh my, you're finally getting it. Now lean back and relax. There's something waiting...

*The Indomitable Silence*

I let my mind go blank as we took a bend in the highway that gradually turned southward along the lake. After cruising along smoothly for some time, enjoying the sun's orange kiss on the rougher and rockier mountains of the southern valley, a scene popped into my mind. A boy was walking in shadows toward a bright white light. In his heart burned a small flame. Alongside the highway people were shouting and trying to push him into the lake. But the boy was determined, and so he focused with all his might and let nobody knock him from his course. From his breast shone a brilliant green that seemed inexhaustible as it expanded in all directions, drowning the derision of the masses. One by one, the naysayers fell quiet and even started to encourage him. The fire in his heart burned more vehemently now, and shadows that had enveloped him vanished. He became one with the light as it shone from within, and in the end there was just him, at peace, with the light, in silence.

Live from the heart, like this boy. Deep within, you'll get glimpses of the divine. You'll cross the point of no return, not as an act of will, but because you've surrendered and embraced the light that can never be taken away. It's always ready when you are.

"And it's that simple?"

It is. I am. You are. Everyone is this pure light in their essence. Just leave those cab'n doors open and you'll never walk alone. Ever.

I swallowed hard, moved by this thought. "Now I just have to remember that in the loudest moments as well as the quietest ones."

Right! Right...

His mind seemed to drift off as we came around a huge cliff that had blocked the sun for the past few minutes. When we came out of the turn, the sun blazed through our windshield, blinding me in an instant. D grabbed his sunglasses and slid them on, transforming

*Out of My Head*

himself into the spitting image of Jack Nicholson. We cruised along without saying a word. By now I was enjoying the drive, the gorgeous weather, and the beautiful scenery. Also, our conversation had turned pleasant and soothing, as he continued to offer many snippets of wisdom with his typical brevity. After some time, I looked over at him. He was smiling, completely at ease, and though I couldn't see his eyes, I could tell they were shining from pure delight. Closing my own, I dozed off … until his voice woke me up.

Check your coat pocket.

"Excuse me? What—?"

Look in the top left pocket.

Barely awake, I opened the flap and peeked inside, feeling a bit like a kid at Christmas. A note! "When did I—?"

I slipped it in there when you had turned away, back at your place. Open it up!

Strangely, I didn't hear the growling of the engine anymore, and yet we were still driving. There seemed to be no end to his magic. Again, my mind went blank. Hearing only the crinkling sound of the unfolding paper, the beating of my heart, and the rush of the wind outside the car, I began to read:

*A day comes in your life when, in the throes of all your pain and suffering, you reach the end of your rope, and a screaming voice cries out loud. You want no more of this! You're done battling the world outside and shutting down the demons inside. You've done everything you could, but it feels like it got you nowhere.*

*The Indomitable Silence*

*Nothing seems to go your way, not even prayer, and you feel forsaken,
hurt, lost. Then, like the blue sky after an outburst of thunder and
lightning, you blink back your stinging tears, lean back and relax,
take a few deep breaths, and begin to see the world
through fresh, clear eyes.*

*You stop dreaming your days away and start to live your dreams, day by day.
You realize your destiny is your making, not your fate, and for the first time
you take your life in your own hands. You're scared but determined,
and you no longer make excuses or feel sorry for yourself.
The victim has died, and the true Self is reborn!*

I finished, folded the sheet tenderly, and looked at D, completely
oblivious to where we were now driving.

This is your chance to awaken to the new you. I wanted to add
that line, by the way. I could feel it in your heart when you went
home that day. But Glider wanted to play, so I got distracted
and forgot. Ha ha.

"So, how…? I didn't write that last part."

Oh, nothing too magical. You left it behind on the pad when you
wrote the first two stanzas, after the waterfall. I simply channeled
what your heart wanted to say. Consider me an occasional co-
writer! Okay, so maybe it is a bit magical. Goes with my job.

"Thank you."

You're very welcome. It had been a while since I had written, so it
felt good. I'm glad I could help your new book project. Now it's up
to you to finish it.

I nodded solemnly and looked out beyond the car, realizing we were
actually entering our driveway! I wondered if Fanny and the girls
had returned. Maybe her car was in the garage. D stopped and put
the car in park. "Okay…"

*Out of My Head*

Hey, I got us from the front door to the car in a flash. I got us back up the valley the same way. Poof! Time and space are like a rubber band, and they're super fun to play with.

We smiled so long at each other that I almost didn't notice his hands were shaking. His frailty seemed to have returned at the thought of parting. "Are you okay to keep driving?"

I'll be fine, bro'. My body is slowly giving up, but I have enough strength to do what I came for, and to get me home. All is well, don't worry.

"Aren't you afraid?"

Afraid of what?

"Dying."

What's there to fear if you've got nothing to lose? I'm at peace, as I know the one who I am isn't going to die, only the one who hosted me for a while. The soul will decide, as you know from your buddies Michael and Atmos. I came into this lifetime when I chose it, and I will leave exactly at the right time. I have no doubt about that.

"I'm gonna miss you."

It's all right. Every time you think of me, know that it's me thinking of you. And every time your heart trembles, know that I am holding it.

"I'll write notes, just as you've done for your three angels."

And I will have read them even before you put pen to paper. But do them anyway. I love notes.

"I love you, brother."

*The Indomitable Silence*

I love you, too. But let's save some of this for later. Though it won't be long now.

He looked me in the eyes, opened up his arms, and we embraced tightly. My heart took one more picture and spoke through controlled sobs, buoyed by a playful thought it had to share: "This car feels like your last chariot, to be born to heaven on the wings of angels! Are you sure you're not some kind of divine being, manifested on the mountain to talk to this earthly guy, just for the fun of it?"

Ha! I'm just a liaison in a Lamborghini.

D gave me a sideways glance and an impish grin, and I got out of the car. When I looked through the window, I saw his hands were steady on the wheel. "Thank you for the ride." He smiled and nodded.

My pleasure. Remember, leave those cabin windows open, and you'll never feel alone, wherever you live. Go to your home now. It's time to be with your family.

I smiled and drummed the door with my fingers. He put the car in gear and in no time zoomed through the front gate. Staring after him for a few moments, I turned and walked up the driveway. The concern I had felt for him was lifted high by what he had awakened in my heart, a deep love for life I now carried with me as I opened the front door and walked in to greet my girls.

# OUR FAREWELL

As I entered the front hall and let my eyes adjust, I more or less expected to be entering D's cabin, knowing him by now to be a tricky old chap. It was with a strange mixture of relief and disappointment that I found myself in my own house. Soon, however, that blend of emotions moved through me, and I hung up my coat and jauntily entered the living room, excited to see everyone. But when I looked around, there was no one there, leading me to conclude D's comment about going to my family was more a courtesy than a product of privileged knowledge on his part. After a few seconds, Cinnamon came running and barking. I petted him for a bit and thought about what to do next.

Shrugging off my disappointment, I made myself a sandwich and a coffee, sat in the living room, and looked out over the late afternoon sun passing unevenly across the valley and city in the distance. Soon a message popped up on my iPhone. Fanny and the girls were grabbing dinner across the lake and might see an early movie. *Okay,* I thought, *I guess it's just me this evening.*

Realizing I could have hung out longer with D and even gone to visit Ray when he dropped off the car, I found myself grumbling. After a few bites, I took my plate back to the kitchen and carried my cup of coffee into the entertainment room. Opening the door, I almost dropped the mug, utterly surprised to find myself in D's cabin! Had my sanctuary of creativity turned into a makeshift portal to the old

*Our Farewell*

man's place?! I found him lying in bed. Glider was on the floor beside him. A small fire was burning in the wood stove.

Welcome back!

"What on Earth…?"

THIS, on Earth!

D was smiling. I wasn't sure whether to laugh or stay annoyed with him. "If you wanted me to be with you, why didn't you just say so?"

Well, I thought you might want to spend some time with your family, and making your whole house my cabin seemed a bit much — a bit selfish.

"But they weren't even there!"

Hey, I'm just a liaison! I can't control what they do. Well, not entirely, anyway. I do have some pull on the other side. But I'm assigned to you, in a manner of speaking, so I'm here for you first and foremost.

"I hope you're not always here. I mean, *here* in my inner sanctum." D coughed out a laugh. He was even worse than I had thought, looking pale and pasty in complexion, his hands shaking quite a bit. Spotting a striped, white woolen blanket on the wooden chest at the foot of his bed, I grabbed it and threw it over him. "Sorry, I was just surprised. Lots of things going on in my mind." His eyes flashed with affection, and I realized how selfish my comment must have sounded. Fortunately, D was bigger than that. He took a deep, painful breath.

My life has been a long journey, but I feel time is drawing near. I am ready.

"I'm not sure I am."

*The Indomitable Silence*

I am always in the cabin. My gift to you. And now your greatest gift is to let me go, in peace.

D's facial expression was now tinged with sadness. "You look sad, though."

In these final days I feel the pain of the world weeping through me. Here in my cabin there's peace, but out there ... all this ignorance, conflict, and vio ence. So much suffering in people's homes. My heart aches for them.

I became quiet and felt how the nearing farewell weighed heavily on me. Our eyes met, and I knew D could see the struggle on my face, but he said nothing. I briefly looked away and cleared my throat. "My heart, too, but mainly because of you." I grabbed my usual wooden chair and brought it near to him, and sat.

Don't be sad for me. Death is not the end, merely a transition to something even more beautiful. And I can't wait to kiss my wife and play with my kids again! Ha, that would be so much fun! Remember the City of Lights?

"Of course! The dancing lights, the life-giving river, my children running over me… How could I ever forget?"

Once I've crossed the line, I hope to do some serious heart-work. I love my solitude, but it's time for the masses to awaken. And I want to be part of that. I want to share the light and warm people's hearts, as this oil lamp has done for me.

He looked at the lamp with such tenderness that it suddenly hit me. The flickering of the light represented his *spirit* — his life force! And, although the lamp was still burning, its light seemed to be weakening, as if his spirit was slowly letting go of him. Yet his voice was still strong.

*Our Farewell*

You see why I'm not sad for myself? There's a lot to look forward to. I only wish I could have stayed a little longer ... with you.

I nodded silently as waves of sadness marched through my heart. Then D turned his face toward me, and I sensed a piece of fatherly advice coming my way.

Please, show people what love is, what love can do. Move them with your stories, your writing. I'll help you, but I can only do so if you don't close the windows to your heart. Speaking of which, open these up!

"Uh ... my windows?"

Oh boy! I mean it literally, of course.

A bit agitated by his snarky response, I got up and opened the windows. As usual, the cool rush of air became warm and soothing, and I found myself calmed by this abiding mystery I now welcomed like an old friend. I was curious about something, however, and asked him: "Why were the windows closed this time?"

Well, I was using some of my last space tricks, but your home theater has no windows, so I was caught off guard a bit in the transition. As you can see, I'm not at my best. Sorry I was a bit grouchy a moment ago, but I am dying after all. Ha ha.

His laughter turned to coughing, and I moved nearer to hold him. Glider looked at us both, whimpering.

No no, it's fine. Thank you. Phew! This is what Mother Earth is feeling right now, but in this case we're the ones doing it to her. Not to mention what we're doing to each other.

It was my turn to make some coffee. I got up, put the kettle on, and started preparing the mugs, while Glider hopped on the bed and

*The Indomitable Silence*

nuzzled in close to D. As I knew this would be the last time we were together, I wanted to take in as much as I could and let him do most of the talking, but some weighty words were already on my lips.

"I think today's tragedies are nothing new. Look at history. Seldom a day has gone by without war or conflict somewhere on this planet. Times have changed, places have changed, technologies have changed, but anger, fear, greed, jealousy, and hatred have always lurked in the dark chambers of people's hearts. Only now, the blood runs around the world and virtually splashes into our faces, as atrocities are shared across the internet and social media in the blink of an eye. I'm afraid *we* haven't changed. We certainly are *not* the fastest learners."

People can be hard-headed ... and a little slow to change. Just like you. Gosh, you're a handful!

His broad smile cleared the space … and my heavy heart. "Thanks, but in all seriousness, we need to pick up the pace. We may be running out of time."

Peace cannot be enforced by rules, laws, or structures; it can only come from how we are within ourselves. And the good thing about a crisis is the heart's cry is so loud that peace will hear its pain and run to its rescue! From within, from the essence of who we are. Yes, I can see the dawn rising. I am hopeful!

D's eyes were burning with intent, and for a moment I forgot how close he was to his last breath. "I hope so, too, but—"

Oh, your intellectual fire is a wonderful instrument, but don't let it be your master. This world has no lack of cleverness. Only of love.

We both remained silent for some time while I finished preparing the coffees. I searched the cooler under the floor and found some packaged cream-filled vanilla and chocolate cakes. They looked … acceptable. Before I could even feel guilty for judging the dessert—

*Our Farewell*

Don't quibble over the cakes. I can sense your lukewarm reaction to them. I know you enjoy fine food, but these will do.

"I didn't say anything. No, they're good. I have … hope!"

Ha! Cheeky till the end, I see. It doesn't matter anyway; about the cake, I mean. I have no appetite, I'm afraid. The coffee by itself will be lovely, thank you.

I found a small table at the head of the bed and pulled it around, and then gathered everything on the tray and returned, placing it all between us. I took a piece of the vanilla cake and we both sipped our coffees, D struggling a bit with his. "I know the open heart is softer and stronger, as you said, but—"

If the heart opens, you feel everything more intensely. Not only love, but also pain. Don't keep stirring the pot. Let the water simply wash over you, like that waterfall we visited, and you'll become the water and the wind, the sun and the earth. Now please pass me a cake, a chocolate one! I'm going to try to get this down.

I passed him the small treat and he managed to chew it. My concerns took over again. "Should I take you to hospital?"

No, I will die where I live. And I will do so AS I've lived — on my own terms!

A surge of pride and invincibility came over me as I listened to D's words, and I knew his words, his presence, would stay with me forever. Soon, however, my curious, inquiring mind was back in the driver's seat. "I never even asked. Maybe out of respect for privacy, or … I don't know. But what exactly are you suffering from? Your ailment, I mean."

*The Indomitable Silence*

Oh! I don't know if there's a category for it, as the medical community would understand. You might say I'm being called back. Some call it "dying of old age," I believe.

"But it's so sudden! I don't understand. There must be something more."

You like your conclusions, don't you? I was like that years ago. It makes me smile.

"They do help me at least try to make sense of the world, and myself."

Make sense? You spent years in your youth whacking a ball over a net! But you did it anyway, and why? Because you loved it! There's no sense when the heart speaks. So please, let me go in my own way. Let me live my truth ... which is certainly not in this cake! Agh, gross!

He tossed the second half of it back on the plate. "Also your truth!" We both laughed. D was suddenly gripped by another fit of coughing. I got up, poured him a glass of water and brought it over. He gulped it down like a desert wanderer, as I had done the other day, and then leaned back in his bed. Taking the glass from him and setting it aside, I saw a man who was totally at ease with himself and his fate. He gazed at me from his reclined position, almost expressionless, until I picked up on a subtle look of serenity mixed with a twinge of concern.

You're still worried about me.

I nodded and looked down at the floor, my hands folded together in front of my knees, trying to avoid his penetrating stare, as I didn't want him to see the tears slowly building behind my eyes.

Look at me!

*Our Farewell*

His stern voice was like a fierce, bracing wind, narrowing my focus to the utmost importance of the moment. I raised my head and, for what felt like an eternity, we took each other in, feeling as one, until I no longer saw him as a frail physical shell but a divine essence transcending the space around us. A fresh breeze passed quickly through the cabin, sweeping the dust from my heart, as D finally spoke.

Do you remember how you felt when you first held Chiara in your arms, and the tears of joy you shed? When you were together with Alyssa, biking through the countryside in your old little village, together, as one heart? Or when you first lay your eyes on Fanny, and you instantly knew she would be your future wife?

I nodded and my heart could smell the perfume of the pictures it had taken at those wonderful moments. "It's all part of me now. How can one forget … love?"

The heart will never forget what it sees through its own eyes. You are. I am. It is...

"A church not made with hands, as Jesus said." D cracked a slow smile of recognition and looked at me, almost expectantly, waiting for more, as Glider returned to his side. Then it came to me. My smile matched his, and I sat up as we said in unison: "A religion of the heart! And its only tenet is love!" The room filled with the familiar green, only this time the atmosphere it created was the most stunning and heartwarming I had ever experienced. D and I basked in its glow awhile, eyes closed, heads down, and hands folded together in silent prayer. Until—

It's been an honor.

*The Indomitable Silence*

Unable to speak, I swallowed, took a deep breath, and raised my chin to honor my friend. The gratitude that boiled up from the bottom of my heart could fill an entire universe. D simply grinned and nodded.

But I'm also tired, so enough talk. Do it!

"Uh… Do what? You always ambush me this way!"

It all starts with one step of surrender to the Now. Do it!

"Again, do…?"

Open the windows and let your heart speak. Don't think. Feel!

My skin bristling with electricity, I looked over my shoulder at the pad and pen sitting in their usual spot. Then it occurred to me what D was urging me to do. I knew how much he had missed his family, but also how he had carried them with him, in his heart. Thinking of my girls now, I wondered how they were doing. *It doesn't have to be complicated,* I could hear him talking through my thoughts. *Start with simple, fatherly love and concern.* Decisively, I downed the rest of my coffee and pulled my chair over, picked up the pen, hunched over the table, and then, with my little angels in mind, the words effortlessly rained down onto the paper:

*In your life people come and go.*
*Some will love you, others will leave you.*
*Some will inspire you, others will challenge you.*
*Some will bless you, others will hurt you.*

*In your life nothing remains the same.*
*Sometimes you feel lost, other times your mission is clear.*
*Sometimes you're scared, other times your faith is as solid as a rock.*
*Sometimes you win, other times defeat is on your side.*

*Our Farewell*

*In your life what you focus on is what you see.*
*Look ahead, but don't forget to look back and learn.*
*Look around, but don't forget to look within and feel.*
*Look up, but don't ever look down on people.*

*In your life every moment can make or break you.*
*Follow your talents, but don't forget strength comes with practice.*
*Follow your passion, but don't forget some things just have to be done.*
*Follow your heart, but don't forget to use your head.*

*In your life you can only walk your journey, not someone else's.*
*Let no one decide where you go, but listen to those who've been there.*
*Let no one decide when you pause, but know you can't live life backwards.*
*Let no one decide when you move on, but take your loved ones with you.*

*Your father will always be there, right beside you.*
*And when you don't see me, my hands are carrying you.*
*And when you don't hear me, my silent voice is guiding you.*
*And when you don't feel me, my heart is giving you shelter.*

*I love you.*
*No matter where you are.*
*No matter where you go.*
*No matter what you do.*
*I love you.*

When I was done, I sat back in my chair, looked at D, and saw the compassion in his eyes for the tears now flowing down my cheeks.

Being human means to cry, and being courageous means you leap willingly into the flowing water.

I dried my face with the heels of my palms. My old friend waited calmly, saying nothing, cuddling with his furry, loyal companion. I tore the top sheet from the pad, folded it carefully, and put it in the

*The Indomitable Silence*

front pocket of my coat. Then, as D continued, I pulled myself back over to his bedside.

And in the waterfall you carve your own pattern through the canyon rock. You never lose yourself by surrendering, my friend.

I recalled an online video of a Muslim man standing in the middle of a big square in Paris. He was blindfolded, holding a sign in front of him: "I am a Muslim and not a terrorist. I trust you. Do you trust me? If so, then please give me a hug." I was moved to see how many people came forward and gave him a hug. Within two days more than twelve million people had seen the clip. From a simple call to what aches within each of us… Of course D had read my mind once more.

People like this man, who are courageous enough to open their wounded heart, will change the world, even if they have to do it one hug at a time.

"Until people get sidelined by some online scandal or sensation, or disheartened and numbed by another horrific event." My sceptical mind had taken over once more, and I could see the pain and effort on D's face as he propped himself up on his elbows to make his next point with greater force. Glider shifted to make room for him, repositioning his little body farther down the bed.

Yes, we are a species of distraction. But people are waking up! Not necessarily through organized religion or formal institutions, but within the intimacy of their homes and communities. Just like we did, here in this little cabin.

"You've given me so much. How can I ever thank you?"

No worries. It makes an old man happy to hear he's been of use — especially to you. Yes, no matter where people meet, it's always the same place, where all are welcome.

*Our Farewell*

"No matter which road we travel and which signposts we follow. I remember that from Michael." D smiled, clearly touched by a fond memory.

The only path that matters is the one that takes you closer to the truth, to that place where—

"The heart sings!" D nodded and gently lay back down on the bed, his expression becoming lighter and more playful, even though his breath was now more labored.

So, why not take a road where you can actually enjoy the ride? Just as we did in our red monster.

Thank you again for that unforgettable experience." D grinned with the satisfaction of a parent who has just given his child the perfect birthday gift. "I'm still amazed how you managed that Italian baby in your condition." He shrugged, weakly raising his hands up in the air.

For heaven's sake, have some fun!

"I'll have to become better friends with Ray, then, and get those keys to that Lamborghini." We both laughed. Then D coughed, and I moved to help him, while Glider whimpered as he looked on. I placed a hand on his shoulder as he drank some more water. After taking the glass from him and setting it down, he grabbed my hand firmly and warmly, and his gaze seemed to bore right into my soul.

Please, take this from an old, dying man. Let go of yesterday, for it is gone. Let go of tomorrow, for it may never come. Seize the day and guard your heart. You've only got one, so keep it pristine! And when you're sad or discouraged, then pray for strength and look up to the stars. Make a wish and think of me. Make your life magical, as I know I have! Thank you, for answering my little note in your mailbox.

*The Indomitable Silence*

D dropped his head to the pillow, closed his eyes, and slowly relaxed his grip on my hands. It wouldn't be long now. Torrents of emotions were running through me, but I wanted to be strong for him, so I choked back my tears and looked outside. The green glow had lit up the room so brightly I hardly noticed night had fallen. There was so much I wanted to say, but the words couldn't break through the clouds of sadness. Instead I kept staring out at the city lights in the distance, listening to the breeze caressing the silence, admiring the strange serenity of the setting. Then, as D opened his eyes, I turned my focus back to him. He tilted his head slightly, taking in the fullness of the moment.

It's okay. My family is waiting for me in the dream that never ends. Your family is waiting for you in the dream that you call reality. So we both have places to go.

My face tightened with grief, and my vocal cords squeezed out an urgent whisper. "But I don't want to leave you alone here." D took a few more deep, painful breaths, and blinked away the growing moisture in his eyes. I placed my other hand over his and squeezed reassuringly. He inhaled once more, and the effort on his face showed how much he wanted to say these final words.

Where I go is not for your eyes, and please don't argue with me on this. Go now, and keep your cabin open at all times, just as I have for you.

We clasped hands one last time. I gently kissed his forehead and then stood up, my legs shaking and my back aching with a sense of impending loss. Yet a mysterious and comforting lightness was starting to dissolve the clouds in my heart and shine through my entire being, helped along by one more quip from D.

Besides, there's no point in us having two annoyed wives — one in heaven and the other one here — so go!

*Our Farewell*

He winked at me. We smiled at each other. "Say hello to Michael and Atmos for me." D nodded. I sensed a flood coming to my eyes, and as the first tear drops fell, I glanced across the room and saw the oil lamp dimming to the point that the flame had almost died, as though to bid me a somber farewell. I turned around slowly and went through the cabin door, ready for whatever room I would find on the other side...

The sensations of intimate familiarity greeted me as I found myself standing in my own bedroom! Traces of green mingled with violet followed me while I moved toward the bed, where Fanny seemed to be in dreamland. Cinnamon lay on the chair beside her. Seeing the glow, he raised his head, but I put my finger to my mouth to shush him. He rested his head back down on his paws. After undressing and easing myself under the covers, I glanced over at the door to see any sign of the cabin beyond. All I could see was the dimness of the room.

So many thoughts were racing through my mind. How would D be? Would he still be alive by morning? And how would I deal with his body, and what would I do with Glider? A companion for Cinnamon? I couldn't even remember how many days I had been with my old friend. Days and nights melted together in my mind. The girls must have been wondering about my oddly timed comings and goings.

My heart, too, was in turmoil, as the effect of the day's powerful emotions had taken their toll. But I remembered D's words. I imagined a cabin inside and opened its windows. *Surrender to the Now,* I told myself over and over, until those wonderful words came to me again, like the soothing voice of a loving parent when you're afraid: *I am the silence. I am the silence. I am...* I closed my eyes and drifted off.

# A NEW DAY

Early morning light announced a new day. Glancing left at the clock beside me, I saw it was 5:30 a.m. Looking to the right, I found my sleeping beauty beside me. Not a yoga day, clearly, but I knew she would be up soon. Not wanting to disturb her, I eased myself out of bed and went to the bathroom.

Staring into the mirror, I saw something I had never really noticed before, or certainly not in quite a while. Despite my sadness that D had likely passed away by now, and the still unanswered question of how I would deal with the situation at the cabin, I detected an ethereal lightness and clarity behind my eyes. Hope and possibility greeted me; somehow everything would be fine. It would be, as my wise friend had said, because I felt it. He was with me. Even the clean, woody aroma of his little home seemed to remain in my nostrils.

Then something peculiar caught my attention. A small shaving cut that must have happened several days earlier was still freshly scabbed on my chin. Of all the strange mysteries over the past several days, however, this paled in comparison. So, I chuckled and went back into the bedroom, where I picked up my coat. Weirdly, all the sheets of writing I had torn off in the cabin were still folded and tucked away in the pocket, not just the recent passage to my girls. I found it odd I hadn't taken the earlier ones out, to enter them in my laptop. My curiosity was then deflected to the fact that my boots were also here, near the bed. Fanny would *not* like that!

*A New Day*

After brushing my teeth, I put on some jeans and a T-shirt, picked up my coat and boots, grabbed my iPhone from the nightstand, and walked softly downstairs, wondering amusedly if I would suddenly find myself in the cabin. Then I recalled what likely awaited me there and felt a wave of apprehension wash through me. Perhaps wanting to delay this inevitability, I set up the coffee machine, placed my boots in the hall, and made my way to the entertainment room. I knew D wouldn't mind. He was likely already with his angels and would want me to write. And yet, something otherworldly about the morning made all assumptions seem up for grabs. I plunked my things down and settled into my favorite chair.

As I flipped my laptop open, the room seemed to close in around me and the world seemed to vanish, as the date in the top right of the screen hit me like a cold wind: it was still November 12! Double checking with my iPhone, I saw this was no joke. It was indeed the same morning I had first gone to meet D in the park! Only 20 minutes had passed since. That all of those moving encounters and wondrous experiences had happened within a twilight dream made my head spin. Yet everything about it felt as true and real as the devices firmly in my hands, or the fresh coffee now brewing in the kitchen.

I hurriedly donned my coat, threw my phone into my pocket, and rushed as quietly as I could to the kitchen. There I grabbed a pad and pen, and wrote a note telling the girls I was going out for a quick morning hike and would be back shortly. Thrusting my feet into my boots, I went through the door into what looked like a crisp, sunny morning similar to those D and I had experienced together. Locking the door behind me, I set off and ran like the wind, the normally hefty boots feeling like winged slippers beneath me as I flew up the mountain toward the cabin.

After many minutes that seemed suspended into one single moment, I came upon the rocks and logs that told me I was getting close. Stopping, I looked down at the ground and focused on my breathing,

*The Indomitable Silence*

trying to distinguish this feeling from everything else I had recently experienced. But it felt no different. This sensation was neither foggy nor incomplete, as most dreams seem when you awaken to a new day and are keenly aware that what you know to be reality stands in clear contrast to the hazy unknown beyond.

I looked up and into the distance. My pulse quickened as my heartbeat knew what my eyes were only now able to discern. There was nothing up ahead! No cabin! D and Glider were gone! My legs became heavy and my heart sank as I labored across the last field toward the empty clearing near the rocky outcrop. Steps slowed even more when I arrived at the site of the cabin. Staring numbly at the spot, I fell to my knees and then crumpled into a ball, numb and lost inside, my only company the cool morning breeze riding along the mountainside.

Time passed; how much, I don't know. Then it came to me. That blessed reminder. That soft and tender grace that enters your being when you are utterly vulnerable and open. I heard D's voice in my heart: *Stand up, reach out, and speak your truth. I am with you.*

Rising to my feet, I looked more closely at the patch of rocky grass where the cabin had been. I didn't even address it as something here or only in my dreams. Telling myself the cabin *does* exist, that it *must* exist, I walked over and looked down. I gasped, pulled the fresh breeze into my lungs, and felt joy run through me as I recognized D's woolen blanket, barely perceptible beneath some thick bramble. I knew he had guided me here.

I reached beneath the scratchy scrub and clutched the blanket lovingly and fiercely. As I lifted it to my chest, I saw there was more. A plastic box with simple words written on top: *Goodbye from an old friend.* My heart rose and broke as I took the box in my hands, opened the top, and looked at its contents: my pad of paper, upon which D had written a final note of farewell. Cradling the box on the blanket like

*A New Day*

a newborn, I walked over to some flat rocks near the outcrop, sat down, and began to read:

> *Hello,*
>
> *Ha! I knew you would be back. Sorry for the shock, but this "assignment" required me to pull up stakes, as they say, and leave few traces behind. I'm still mastering mind and matter beyond time and space, but I'm getting there. And when you read this, I will already be here with my loved ones. Be happy for me and don't be sad. Always remember the beautiful moments and conversations we had, and the dream we shared. Know that I'm never far away. Although you may not see me, I do see you. I see the beauty in your soul, the light in your heart, and I feel all that you feel. I'm right here, just a heart's thought away. All I want is to see you happy. And when you feel lost or alone, just think of me and I'll be there, right beside you. We are together, always. I love you.*

The words echoed within me. I looked up, staring searchingly at nothing in particular. Blinking away the blur of tears, I focused hard on the now empty spot. I imagined it as my own heart, open and ready to find D at any time. My skin jumped with goosebumps and my chest filled as the cabin seemed to materialize before my very eyes! There it was! *You see what you believe*, I thought to myself. Breathlessly, I continued to read:

> *I know you've always wondered who I really am, this apparently homeless guy living in a remote cabin with his playful, furry companion. The man who went, simply, by the letter D. I hope you're sitting now, likely by the rocky outcrop. I am Daniel, your beautiful middle name. I am you, and you are me! That's why*

*everything felt so familiar and why I knew so much about your life, your work, your writing. I came to you from beyond time and space, where I live in the realm of infinite possibility. You may already have seen the cabin appear out of thin air, because we share the same heart. This is why I came, to awaken your light and to give you a bit of this heavenly magic. Of course, I changed my appearance to do all this. Ha ha!*

I looked up again. The cabin was still there, shimmering in the rising sun, which was now fully up over the distant east mountains. Swallowing hard, I shook my head in baffled delight. Then a darker thought came to me. What about my family? I looked northward over my left shoulder, to where I had seen the crosses. Too far to see from here. I continued reading:

*I know you're concerned about your family. But please don't worry, because what you've experienced was only a dream created in my heavenly workshop to help you seek the indomitable silence, listen to your heart's fierce whisper, feel how precious life is, and know that true love never ends. What you've learned before, with Michael and Atmos, is still true. Nothing is set in stone, the future is open, and the soul still has many options to choose from.*

*So don't mourn my death, as I am still here, and your family is just fine, as we all come and go from heaven a little every day. Neither will your hopes, dreams, and passions ever die if you let the heart guide you to your full potential. Never allow your spirit to be buried under the burdens of life. Shine as only you can shine. Dance as only you can dance. Sing as only you can sing. You are beautiful just the way you are.*

*A New Day*

> *All is well, my dear soul brother. Never stop writing, reaching, laughing, learning, and loving. Now go and finish your book! Touch hearts. Create opportunities. And never stop believing.*

> *With love, your fierce whisper, D.*

Now weeping with joy, I let my arms and shoulders go limp, as I surrendered to the full wonder of the moment; to the realization that all would indeed be okay. Fear and confusion passed through me and disappeared down the valley. In the distance I could hear the rush of the waterfall we had peered into together. Smiling, because I knew it was too far to be perceived with eyes and ears alone, I now saw the world as a place to create in pure joy as a child might. A place to love and dance. A place to be truly myself!

The vision of the cabin slowly faded, replaced by a broad band of sunlight that was growing as the mountainside fully welcomed the morning. Absently caressing the pad, I began chuckling, and soon I was laughing aloud at the utter thrill of being alive, of having been given so many gifts that now, without the blinding veil of troubled thoughts, were so clearly evident and available to me.

Strength of purpose filled my limbs as a deep breath filled my lungs. I placed the pad back into the box, closed the top, and stood tall. Then, glancing at the cabin's site once more, I turned and walked home, my heart at peace, the soft breeze in my hair and at my back.

~

I opened the door, relieved to find it was my actual home. Not that I hadn't enjoyed D's space tricks, but it was time to be with my family. What a delight it was to be greeted by them all, including Cinnamon, who was barely able to contain himself. The entire house was in a state of heightened enthusiasm and rich with the aroma of food. The

*The Indomitable Silence*

first was Chiara, always bold and insistent when she has something to say. I placed the box and blanket on the front hall table, and covered them with my coat, as my eldest ran to me.

"Dad, Dad — you've got to listen to this! I had such a weird dream last night. We were speeding down the valley in a red Lamborghini. You were in the passenger seat, and I was kind of floating above the car. The driver — he looked sort of familiar. I'm not sure ... older guy, blue eyes. But I was with you all the way, as if I could read your thoughts. I can't remember them now. You seemed really content and happy, though, which is good, because, you know, you've been a little distracted lately. It was awesome, but strange! Everything was so real, and yet somehow I knew I was dreaming. Ever get that?"

My eyes widened and I smiled, as a soft warmth filled my chest. "That is amazing, sweetie! Perfect dream for you, being such a car lover." I took her in my arms and tried to give her a big hug.

"Oh, Dad!" She gave me her usual teenage resistance and pulled away, feeling awkward with the unexpected display of affection. I laughed, happy to see her as she truly is. "Come on," she said. "Mom's got breakfast going."

We walked out into the open living area. Alyssa was reading a textbook on the sofa. Fanny was in the kitchen; the dining room table was set for a quick breakfast of scrambled eggs and toast, with a bit of fruit. I said good morning to the two of them, as Chiara took a seat on one of the kitchen stools and checked her phone.

"Hi, Dad," Alyssa said in her quiet, gentle voice. She looked at me and smiled mysteriously. Something was on her mind, I could tell. "I had an odd dream, too."

"Oh?" I moved over and sat beside my youngest on the sofa. "And what was yours about?"

*A New Day*

"Hm. Let's see. I was out for a walk, up the mountain a bit, when I found this funny little cabin. There was a cute doggie outside. I remember petting him. But it was strange, Dad. I saw you go in, but you didn't knock. You just walked in like you had been there before. I could tell by your face you were happy and calm, so I didn't call you. I looked through the window and saw a tall man — like you, but older. He wore boots and a jacket. He seemed friendly, a bit solitary, and a little goofy — like you are sometimes."

"Oh!" I grabbed her and gave her a hug. She giggled. "Not like you, hey!"

"But he was also smart, I could tell, and you two talked a lot, and then sometimes disappeared, leaving coffee and sweets on the table. I don't know what you two talked about, but it was a cozy cabin, with a lamp burning in one of the corners. Funny, I've never seen anything up that way on our walks, but in this dream it seemed so real! I liked it. There was more, like all of us were in a beautiful city ... and this river, but I can't remember that part now."

"Yes!" exclaimed Chiara, looking up from her phone. "I also remember flying over a city — when I wasn't flying over the Lamborghini! Lots of lights, and the food was great, too." She chuckled with satisfaction.

I looked at my two girls, and my whole being felt tingly and alive with the perfume of happiness. Alyssa and I smiled at each other, while Chiara grinned and shrugged. Then, instinctively, I turned to Fanny as she spoke.

"Also real is the fact that you left your coat and boots upstairs in the bedroom last night after you went out!" she shouted in playfully scolding Dutch. I smiled, realizing now why D was so easy with the language. It was me! "Where were you? Then you were gone this morning. And a paper note instead of using your iPhone? Are you okay?"

206

*The Indomitable Silence*

I got up and walked over to my wife, put my arm around her, and kissed her softly on the cheek. A faint smile appeared on her face as she waved me away. "Breakfast is ready. We don't have much time before school. Girls!" Grinning, I found a mug and filled it with coffee.

We gathered around the dining room table, and its wooden beauty reminded me... I sat and looked at my cherished ones. We ate silently for some time, enjoying the food, though I could tell there was a collective secret hovering over the table. Next it appeared to be Fanny's turn. After finishing her mango, she paused with her fork suspended in the air, and looked at me, question marks all over her face.

"Seems it was a bizarre night all around. I had a dream about an older man, too." My heart quickened a bit now, as I knew my wife was not so inclined to flights of fancy, and I was curious to hear her experience. "We were dancing in a large hall, kind of like the one where we first met in that discotheque." My girls looked at her, and then at each other. I knew they had been aware of our marital difficulties lately. Their mother continued. "We danced. It was very nice. Then you disappeared through a door." I wanted to correct her and say she had *led* me through it, but I restrained myself. "Then, right away, this older gentleman came in from the street. He was tall, like you, and nicely dressed; had bright blue eyes. Lovely man. He said I need not worry, and that you had a few things to take care of. And that you would be back soon. Then he took my hand and twirled me under the lights. Very smooth, I have to say. Then he smiled, bowed to me, and followed you through that door. Very unusual dream!"

The four of us looked at each other and my heart expanded to the size of the room. "What a lovely dream," I said to her. We exchanged a quick smile, and we all continued eating. Then it was my turn.

*A New Day*

"Remarkable! Seems like a household dream. So, then, did any of you catch this mystery man's name?"

All three answered in exact unison, as though simultaneously struck by an epiphany: "Daniel!"

I burst into uncontrollable laughter, my body heaving with guffaws. A bit startled, they searched each other's faces and then began laughing with me, as they all recognized it was one of my middle names. Cinnamon scampered toward the table, barking at the sudden surge in energy.

"Shh, Cinnamon! It's okay." I friskily ruffled his fur as the joyous roar around the table gradually subsided. "It seems you all met my middle name in your dreams!"

"And your middle name dances better than you, my dear!" Fanny teased, making the girls burst into unbridled laughter again.

Smiling, I looked at her steadily and lovingly. "Well, dreams are not only magical but can also be, in a sense, quite real. A play of possibilities. God's way of showing us who we truly are — or who we can become." I put my hand on hers and we shared a tender, wordless exchange with our expressions.

"Oh Dad!" Chiara said with an attempt at teenage dismissiveness, but I could see in her eyes a deeper acknowledgement of something more special than she would have liked to admit. Alyssa said nothing, lost in thought. She finished her breakfast and took her plate to the kitchen.

"And what about our little dreamer?" Fanny asked, tilting her head curiously toward me as I released her hand and reached for my coffee. "Did this man visit you too?" I took a sip and squinted with mock consideration.

*The Indomitable Silence*

"You know, after my walk last night, I was in a funny mood. Distracted, as Chiara said. I remember someone. He was like an ... old friend or something. He told me I should get my coat and boots out of the bedroom before you woke up." I snorted and chuckled.

Fanny smiled and faked an eye roll, getting up from the table. "Okay, girls, let's get ready. It's getting late."

Chiara shot me a quick grin and got up. She grabbed her phone and bag as Alyssa walked over and gave me a big hug, before going for her own bag. They both busied themselves with last minute preparations for school. I watched them all move around, filled with gratitude for the moment and for all the beauty they have brought into my life. After a minute or so, I got up and went to the kitchen. I grabbed Fanny by the shoulders, looked her in the eyes, and said, "I love you."

"I love you, too," she whispered softly.

I gave her a tender kiss. "I'm going to do some work now."

"Okay, love, I'll see you later."

As I left the kitchen, my eyes fell upon the fruit bowl on the side counter. Right in the middle was a plump, red apple. Grinning, I picked it up and held it aloft in the morning sunlight. I noticed a small brown patch and rubbed it with my thumb. "*Perfect*," I whispered to myself, and continued across the dining room. "See you, girls, have a nice day!"

When I got to the front hall, I gingerly lifted the box, blanket, and coat, and made my way into my sanctuary. As I set the bundle on the bar counter behind the theater seats, I heard Chiara call from the front hall: "Dad, I think you dropped something." I rushed back and found her clutching the small pile of my writings, which must have fallen from my coat pocket. She had one open and was reading it: "'*I am the silence...*'"

*A New Day*

"Here, sweetie, thank you!" I reached toward her hands, smiling in anticipation of a smart-ass remark I knew would be coming.

"You are the silence?" She began laughing as I took the papers from her. "Silence is not what I hear from my bedroom when you play all that junk late at night while I'm trying to study. Oh, you call it music, I'm sorry."

"Well, it's not necessarily meant to be silence in the literal sense, but the calm you sometimes feel in your heart."

"Dad, really? Ugh! Adults are so lame."

"Feel free to practice some literal silence yourself right now, young lady! And you're running late for school."

"Fine." She rolled her eyes as I gave her a playfully triumphant grin, folded the open sheet, and sorted the others into a tidy pile in my palm. She turned and rushed upstairs.

"Love you." I chuckled and then returned to my "junk room", as she had so lovingly called it. Usually I would close the door behind me for privacy, but not this time. Instead I left it wide open as I entered my cherished space. My laptop was where I had left it earlier, waiting for my return. I slowly grabbed the box and brought it to my chair along with my writing. Settling in with my feet up, I placed my faithful comrade on my legs. So much had happened that I wasn't sure where to begin. But inspiration was not far away, as D seemed to be calling out to me again. Opening the box, I took out the pad and flipped past the first pages I had already read. Then I found additional words he had clearly expected me to find later:

> *Hello again, my friend!*
>
> *It may seem odd calling yourself that way, but hey, you must be friendly toward yourself. After all, who will*

*The Indomitable Silence*

*hear the whisper in your heart when all sounds have faded, and catch the tears falling down when all lights have died? We share the same heart, you and I. That's the beauty of love. Speaking of sharing, did you enjoy how your family was in touch with our experience through their dreams? Ha ha. That required a great deal of my skill level, so I'm glad it worked! By now you're likely sitting in your inner sanctum, wondering where to begin the next part of your quest. Well, I couldn't move on to the other side without offering you a handy guiding recap of what we've talked about on that magical mountain. Remember as you continue writing that we are one, so these thoughts are also yours...*

### *Choices for a Life Well Lived*

*As I hear the breath of heaven waiting to free me from my earthly body, I reflect upon my life. I know many would consider it to have been a success, but my good fortune is not what I'm thinking of right now. It may all have been nice for a while, but it's meaningless when eternity is staring you straight in the eyes. Wealth and material success is not what you should pursue, as it may turn you into a twisted being, like I was for too long. God gave you a heart not to lose it in greed or fear, but to use it to love one another. This love is all you take with you when returning to your heavenly home. So, my dear friend, you came to me with a mind wide open, and I leave you to this earthly journey knowing your heart is wide open, too. Mission accomplished!*

*I want to leave you with a set of choices that will ultimately decide the quality of your life. Choices*

*A New Day*

*that either take you closer to the heart or further
away from it. Choices that determine not only your
well-being, but also that of every heart you touch on
this troubled and wonderful planet. So choose wisely.*

*Choose to be compassionate, yet don't allow others to tread upon you.
Choose to be generous, yet don't give to wolves in sheep's clothing.
Choose to be the light, yet don't ignore the dark side of life.
Choose to be positive, yet don't lose sight of reality.*

*Choose to be humble, yet don't feel inferior.
Choose to be happy, yet don't think life is a constant high.
Choose to be loving and caring, yet don't claim anyone to be yours.
Choose to be adventurous and playful, yet don't walk away from yourself.*

*Choose to enjoy the moment, yet don't neglect the work that needs to be done.
Choose to learn from the past, yet don't take yesterday with you.
Choose to laugh a lot, yet know that tears heal the soul.
Choose to praise, yet be genuine when you speak.*

*Choose to live by choice, not by chance.
Choose to count your blessings, not your tears.
Choose to use the head well, but live from the heart.
Choose to accept reality, but always do the best you can
to create the life you want. Make it magical, as I know I have!*

I took a deep and slow breath, fully aware of the freedom of choice
I had. As I exhaled, I sensed his reassuring presence, just as he had
promised. I felt he was with me, and I knew all I needed to move
forward toward whatever the future would hold for me and my family
was already within. I just had to make the right choices, not only for
me but also for our shared heart.

I sat in sublime silence, which soon mingled with the hurried sounds
of my beloved family throughout the house. It all flowed through me

*The Indomitable Silence*

and I smiled, for I knew yesterday and tomorrow could not conquer this wonderful moment. Nor could time take away the powerful love and gratitude I felt within. I closed my eyes and a single tear rolled down my cheek.

After what seemed an eternity, I opened my eyes to the waiting screen. As usual, I grabbed the remote control and turned the system on. Music filled the room, like the soundtrack of my heart, guiding me into the wondrous unknown. Holding my willing fingertips over the keyboard, I looked up, smiled broadly, and whispered, "Thank you, D."

# GOODBYE

Dear reader,

Thank you for taking this journey with me. While it may seem our paths go different ways from here, the truth is that the inward quest always brings us back together. The deeper we go and the higher we fly, the more we feel the One Light shine through our heart. We will meet again, in that place where we can taste the sweetness of love, smell the fragrance of freedom, and hear the fierce whisper of the indomitable silence in all of us. A state of being where we can be One with the divine Heart of everything, where our magical Self lives and awakens in a never-ending dream.

I did finally finish the "A day comes..." passage I started in that magical cabin. I will leave it with you now, as I lay down my pen, knowing that, although this is a work of fiction, the words speak the truth of my heart. We all create our own stories day by day. Be sure yours is one of love and wonder. And then share it as you walk bravely through life, making the Heart of the world as beautiful as you are in your most blissful dreams. Just as D did.

*A day comes in your life when, in the throes of all your pain and suffering, you reach the end of your rope, and a screaming voice cries out loud. You want no more of this! You're done battling the world outside and shutting down the demons inside. You've done everything you could, but it feels like it got you nowhere.*

*Goodbye*

*Nothing seems to go your way, not even prayer, and you feel forsaken,
hurt, lost. Then, like the blue sky after an outburst of thunder and
lightning, you blink back your stinging tears, lean back and relax,
take a few deep breaths, and begin to see the world
through fresh, clear eyes.*

*You stop dreaming your days away and start to live your dreams, day by day.
You realize your destiny is your making, not your fate, and for the first time
you take your life in your own hands. You're scared but determined,
and you no longer make excuses or feel sorry for yourself.
The victim has died, and the true Self is reborn!*

*You know you can't control everything, nor everyone, and
that fear and worry isn't going to make life easier,
and soon the breath of peace and joy
whispers the heart's surrender.*

*You accept you're not perfect and that your life
may never be exactly the way you want it to be,
and soon the breath of peace and joy
whispers the heart's acceptance.*

*You recognize there's so much you don't know and can't do, so you
identify with nothing, not even your highest accomplishments,
and soon the breath of peace and joy
whispers the heart's humility.*

*You realize everyone has their own path to walk and that
it's not someone else's purpose to make you happy,
and soon the breath of peace and joy
whispers the heart's compassion.*

*You learn the importance of mutual respect and that
two people united can accomplish more than one,
and soon the breath of peace and joy
whispers the heart's connection.*

*The Indomitable Silence*

*You stop complaining, blaming, or judging others for what*
*they do or who they are, or for expectations not met,*
*and soon the breath of peace and joy*
*whispers the heart's understanding.*

*You stop taking yourself too seriously and you learn to laugh*
*at the mistakes you make, knowing they are part of life,*
*and soon the breath of peace and joy*
*whispers the heart's humor.*

*You no longer dwell in your tears, but instead you count your blessings,*
*even in times of trial and hardship, when all hope seems lost,*
*and soon the breath of peace and joy*
*whispers the heart's gratitude.*

*You see life as a journey and that no matter where you go, it's the full*
*engagement and commitment that brings a sense of purpose,*
*and soon the breath of peace and joy*
*whispers the heart's passion.*

*You learn to surround yourself with people who*
*bring forth the best in you, not the worst,*
*and soon the breath of peace and joy*
*whispers the heart's love.*

*You come to know the one who you really are,*
*not the one who you thought you were,*
*and soon the breath of peace and joy*
*whispers the heart's "I am."*